Chapter One

Emily

Emily wandered to the window and smudged glass into the greyness beyond. A gust of wind howled between the trees in the garden sending a flurry of autumnal colours spinning onto the sodden grass.

"Sometimes I wish I could turn back the clock," she said to herself as she looked into the heaviness of the day, pulling the hot coffee mug into her chest.

The nutty aroma filled her lungs with a warming hug as she closed her eyes and drifted back to the distant haziness of the seemingly endless summers of her carefree youth. Magical evenings filled with laughter and dancing with lost friends as the scent of wild thyme and jasmine had intoxicated the warm evening air. Watching and hearing nothing but the chirping sound of the cicadas, as the setting sun had displayed a palate of vibrant colours over the watery horizon, capturing her soul. Endless lazy days on warm golden sands submersed in its heady coastal air entirely hypnotised by the sounds of perfectly formed turquoise waves crashing against the shore. The warmth of the Greek sunshine that had kissed her skin and sent shivers of bliss through her relaxed body. Those moments before her understanding of normality had been sucked from her very existence.

A sudden crashing noise jolted her back to the present moment and to the drizzly misery of late September in the UK. Taking a sip from her mug, Emily watched through the raindrops as two men struggled against the wind. Fighting against the elements to pick up a wheelie bin that had toppled over in its strong unforgiving gusts. She continued to watch as they emptied its decaying contents into the back of the refuse lorry. Days like these made reality a bit harder to cope with. Being cooped up with nothing to distract her mind made Emily mull over the events of the past few weeks. She still could not quite make sense of precisely what had happened. It was still almost too crazy to be real.

Emily turned her gaze from the window and wandered across to the well-loved sofa bed that filled the compact living space of her dreary room. She flopped herself into its perfectly formed seat pads, shaped over the years by her overly ample buttocks. Then, she curled her legs up and took another sip of coffee. Her mobile suddenly burst into life with the spine-chilling, melodic reminder of its sender. Taking out her phone, she read yet another grovelling text to add to the several messages she had already received that morning from her ex-boyfriend, Jake.

"Are you being serious? After everything we've been through together, you can't even be bothered to answer my calls or messages. One bad mess up and that's you done!"

This wasn't one terrible mess up. This had been the biggest mess-up of the century. Jake had utterly screwed with her mind and she wanted nothing more to do with him. Emily threw her mobile onto the empty seat beside her and glugged down the last of the coffee.

Flicking on the TV, she searched through the listings looking for anything to fill the morning void. Settling on "Homes under the Hammer," her mind was blissfully distracted for a few pointless minutes, as she watched the transformation of a dilapidated old council house to the perfect family home.

A knock at the door interrupted the crucial part where they gave a new value on the completed project. Standing up in a moment of frustration, Emily wandered the dimly lit hallway. She opened the door to a sweaty, red-faced and overweight deliveryman, awkwardly holding a bouquet of red roses and a bottle of Dom Perignon Champagne while trying to catch his breath.

"I...have a...delivery for...Miss Emily White." He paused, trying to regain control of his breath. "Could you...sign here... please?" he managed to blurt out between wheezes, then extending his digital signing pad into her empty hands. "Thanks!" he said as he thrust the delivery into her arms, swivelled on the spot, walked towards the first of eleven flights of stairs and reluctantly started his descent.

Emily momentarily remained in the doorway with her arms filled with the half-expected gift. She knew exactly who it was from without even needing to check the card. This is what he did. He always thought he could buy her forgiveness, but this time he had gone too far. After everything she had found out, there was no going back.

Taking the handwritten gift card out of the flowers, Emily placed the bouquet next to a full glass bottle of creamy milk on her elderly neighbours doorstep. Knocking their door, she wandered back into her flat. Putting the cold bottle of expensive champagne into an empty space in the wooden wine rack on top of the fridge freezer, she opened the small pink envelope and read the card.

"I am really sorry. Please forgive me. J X"

"Urgh!!" she grunted disapprovingly.

Pushing the pedal on the chrome waste bin, Emily threw the card inside and slammed it shut. Why couldn't he just leave her alone, she thought, as her mobile pinged again with yet another message from Jake.

"Do you like the flowers? I thought we could share the champagne tonight over dinner so I can explain? 7pm at mine?" his text read.

Emily had no intention of going anywhere near his house ever again. His money didn't impress her. His extravagant gifts, last minute holidays and meals out at expensive restaurants were just a distraction from the real Jake that she now knew. The Jake who had lost her, her job, her sanity and the reason why she was flat-sharing with creepy Colin, who only came out at night.

In actual fact, she didn't even know what her flat-mate looked like. He silently wandered about in the darkness of the early hours and never emerged from his room by day. The only reason Emily knew he had existed was that she had seen his shadow move from under the crack of his bedroom door as she had darted past on the way to the loo. She had become accustomed to sleeping with her door-locked and had added several additional bolts for extra protection. She even kept a water pistol of garlic-infused water next to her bed just in case she was actually living with Count Dracula himself.

Emily hated where she lived. Her old home and life had been just perfect. Her voice had graced the screens in every living room in the UK and beyond, on the numerous adverts that had blurted out from their devices or the audiobooks people listened to on a late-night drive home or whilst they drank cocoa before bed. She was famous, yet unknown. It was the most perfect combination. Her generous salary had afforded her a luxury rented flat in a highly sought-after area, overlooking the local park's green lushness. She had decorated the flat with matching furnishings from her hard-earned income and had spent so many pleasant evenings watching the setting sun from her balcony as the world went by. She had been so content and life had been so uncomplicated.

Emily had been single for almost a year after her childhood romance with her first boyfriend and love of her life, Tom, had come to an abrupt end. They had been an item since Year 10 at school. After almost nine years together, they had split after a stupid disagreement while on a gap year holiday, fruit harvesting in Greece. They had argued and she had acted stubbornly by booking a one-way ticket home, leaving Tom broken hearted. That was the last time she had seen him. After several weeks of trying to contact him to apologise and stalking him on social media, he had deleted his account and disappeared from society. Tom had remained one of her biggest regrets.

Her relationship with Tom had been the perfect experience of young love. Those exciting and awkwardly innocent "first moments" that they had shared. The first kiss. The first innocent gropes. Even first-time sex that had been military planned for weeks and had taken place in Tom's typical teenage boy's bedroom, while his mum had popped to his Aunty Carol's for her usual Friday night out. No romance, no seduction, no experimenting. Just missionary position that they had seen in a dodgy porn magazine that Tom had bought to get tips ahead of their scheduled night of passion. With Irresistible by Beyoncé playing in the background, she lost her virginity in a few measly minutes after an embarrassing struggle in complete darkness to put on the condom. It had not been the "out of this world" experience that she had hoped for. But, after that night, they had been at it like rabbits finding any chance to sneak off to satisfy their raging hormones. Then after finishing school and the trials of a long distance relationship whilst they had both studied at university, they had both decided to runaway on a gap year that had lasted a lot longer than planned. These were childhood memories that would remain special to her for her lifetime.

She had not been looking for romance. Emily was happy working the usual 9 to 5, then partying the weekends away with her friends at their regular haunts and living it up on expensive annual holidays that her wage easily supported. She had bagged a few drunken one-night stands. After waking up to some really unattractive sights, she had managed to sneak away without waking each conquest. In one of her figure-hugging outfits, with makeup smudged down her hungover face and clutching her killer heels, Emily had taken the walk of shame home several times. She was happy playing the field and having fun. The last thing she wanted was anything serious.

Then Jake had happened. After a chance meeting at an exclusive bar, a cheesy chat up line that she had initially ignored, a mutual love of gin, and an evening of being completely charmed by his compliments, Emily had buckled and reluctantly agreed to a date. The date had gone better than she could have ever imagined. They chatted non-stop all evening and seemed to have so much in common. He had received her complete empathy when he told her that he had not long split up with his controlling crazy ex. She had accused him of being the unfaithful one, while all the time she had been having an affair with his best friend. After he had ended things with her, she had become obsessed with him. Stalking his every move before finally attacking him with a knife one evening as he had arrived home from a night out with friends. He had lifted his shirt to show the scars from the attack across his perfectly toned torso.

Emily had been in fits of laughter with stories of his experiences of famous people he had befriended in high society circles. His tales of the high adrenaline sports he pursued and various high-end holiday resorts he had travelled to excited Emily. She actually felt she had met her perfect match. After too many varieties of gin and a ridiculously expensive bottle of Chateau Le Pin, he had literally charmed the pants off her and they had ended up having the most incredible night of passion back at his expensive hotel suite.

Jake literally swept her off her feet with his attention. Their romance had her head floating in clouds for months. Her friends had noted her lack of attendance at their regular weekend meets. She had no desire to spend mid-week nights alone in her perfect home. She was spellbound by the excitement this new relationship had injected into her life. Jake would whisk her away on city breaks all over Europe. He was the most perfect gentleman rejecting any payment she offered towards the expensive restaurant bills and luxury apartments they stayed in. She woke to breathtaking vistas over the various cityscapes that twinkled in the evening sunsets. She had been thrust into a lavish lifestyle that she could only ever dream of affording.

And the sex was out of this world. Emily had suddenly become a bit of a whore. Instead of demanding the lights out for a quick romp in missionary position, she found herself taking crazy risks in the most public of places just to please Jake. Going down in the elevator had taken on an entirely new meaning.

Jake also showered her with gifts. Every week a new Pandora charm, designer handbag or expensive pair of Jimmy Choo's would arrive at her doorstep. A dozen red roses were hand-delivered with yet another gift card exposing yet another surprise weekend getaway every Friday. Her life had changed so dramatically, and she had quite unexpectedly fallen head over heels for Jake.

But as time wore on, the gifts became less exciting, the trips monotonous, and Emily felt little in control of her own life. She yearned for a quiet night alone, watching a cheesy rom-com with a Dominoes pizza. The thought of packing yet another weekend bag for yet another city break, and having to get glammed up for another Michelin star restaurant, irritated her. All Emily wanted was a night out with her girlfriends and a bit of normality to her life.

She had not been out with the gang in months and, fed up with her constant rejections, they had stopped asking her to join them. During a weekend stay in Paris and over another expensive meal at the opulent "Le Pre Catelan," home of the famous French Chef, Frederic Anton, she had brought the subject up. As the veal sweetbreads had melted on her palate, Jake had ranted about her being ungrateful, selfish and spoilt. A vein running down his forehead pulsated with a wave of anger that Emily had never witnessed before as his eyes bulged with rage.

This had erupted into their first-ever argument and Emily rushing out of the restaurant, as elegantly as possible. Clutching at her killer designer heels and dabbing at her tears with the restaurant's expensive embroidered napkin, she had hailed a taxi back to the hotel. When Jake had eventually caught up with her, Emily had pretended not to hear him arrive. She remained motionless under the covers in the darkness of the suite. She kept her eyes shut as he tried hard to apologise with his usual seduction tactics. His advances had been rejected and he had rolled over with a disapproving huff.

The following day she had been woken to a bouquet of flowers and two front row tickets to watch her favourite band in Rome a few months later. This had been the first time he had wooed her with his apologetic gifts. After this, his attention became more intense, the arguments became more frequent, and the gifts more extravagant.

But Emily still wanted a little freedom to see her friends. After going on a sex strike for a few days, Jake eventually gave in and agreed that she could go out, on the understanding that he would be her taxi there and back. But, when she did plan to go out, Jake would create an argument about her figure-hugging clothes. He would accuse her of going out on "the pull" and demand that she change into something more suited to her age.

Emily was still only in her twenties and had an enviable figure that she worked hard to achieve at the local gym. She followed fashion devoutly and wanted to wear the clothes that she felt suited her voluptuous toned figure. She didn't want to hide away her youth in middle-aged clothes that her mother would wear. Her appearance was becoming an issue. Emily reminded him that he had been attracted to the way she dressed and her sexy curves so she shouldn't have to stop dressing as she pleased because he was insecure. Plus a full new wardrobe would be expensive and she could not afford it. Jake had argued that he was only looking out for her welfare and she should compromise a little. It had nothing to do with his insecurities.

Jake had taken her on yet another surprise weekend trip to London and, as a way of apologising, took her clothes shopping. Scrutinising everything she picked up and, after trying on so many different outfits that met his approval, he paid for a completely new wardrobe. He had gone for the sexy city chic trouser suits and heels of high powered women, which he said had turned him on. This control had given him a surge of pleasure, resulting in an erection and, even after her objections, had ended up having a quickie in the changing room of Harrods. This was the first time that she had actually felt like his possession rather than his partner.

Then, from nowhere, she had been made redundant from her dream job. She spent weeks trawling through online job websites and updating her professional experience on Linked in, hoping to find a similar role. After lots of knock backs and a bit of perseverance, Emily had succumbed to financial pressures. She found a temporary job working shifts in a local call centre. It wasn't perfect, but it brought in the needed income to pay her rent and bills.

Jake had belittled her new role and offered to support her. At the same time, she could search for something more worthy of her capabilities. Emily had refused politely and accepted the position, maintaining her financial independence. The downside to her new job was she had to work some late shifts and the occasional weekend as per her team roster. Jake had not liked the challenging constraints her new job put on their relationship.

Yet Emily had loved her new job. It gave her a social life again and loads of new friends to hang out with after work. After her Saturday evening shift, she would head straight to the pub and then, onto a nightclub, staggering in just as the sun rose and the birds sang their morning chorus. There would be an unhealthy amount of missed calls and messages from Jake on her mobile, some pleasant and concerned, others vile and accusing. Emily would just turn off her phone and flop on the bed, surfacing just as the sunset. She was finally starting to feel in control of her life again.

Her behaviour angered Jake. He felt that she was being selfish and not considering his needs in their relationship. He would always bring up that the weekends should just be for the two of them and not for her to be out partying as if she was single. Even after Emily had invited him to join her and her new friends after work, Jake had refused. This had started to form a wedge between them. Emily had tried to end things with Jake on several occasions, but he had a way of reeling her back almost as if she was under some kind of magic spell. She fell for his pleads, promises and lies every time. Even after telling her that things would change and he would be more trusting, they never did. After a few days, he would be back to his usual self, and the emotional bullying would start again.

Having been in her new role for a few weeks, Emily was into the swing of life in the call centre. The office banter, the gossip and the drama that unfolded through the working week were almost like watching a TV soap. The office affairs that went on were enough to give Eastenders a run for its money. Emily couldn't keep up with the lunchtime flings that were happening all around her. Flirting couples would disappear to take "lunch" together and return grinning from ear to ear. The next day the same guy would leave with a different girl. It was almost like watching sushi on the conveyor belt, taking their pick from the various dishes that tempted their taste buds that day.

But Emily was never tempted, regardless of the attention from the guys in the office. Even some of the girls had made a pass, but she would never be unfaithful to Jake, no matter how much he irritated her. She would end things if she ever thought that she was tempted by one of the many hot men that she rejected weekly. Yet Jake would constantly accuse her of being unfaithful or flirting with her colleagues. If she came out of the office with her shirt button undone, revealing a little too much of her cleavage, Jake would accuse her of infidelity. Emily was starting to despise the situation she was in and started to noticeably withdraw from the relationship. That's when things had taken a different turn. That's when Jake became desperate.

Chapter Two

Jake

Jake hated being single. His recent girlfriend had been an absolute lunatic. She had broken up with him after catching him out texting several girls from an online dating site. He had denied everything, of course, as it was only a bit of fun. He had not been unfaithful, as he had never actually met any of them. Anyway, she deserved what she got. He had a right to chat with a few other girls to keep him company while she was out on the pull with her mates. With those slutty clothes that she wore, she had obviously wanted to reel in her next victim. He didn't need her anyway. He could have anyone he wanted. Girls were always falling at his feet with his designer clothes, expensive watches and his charming ways.

He sipped at his drink and watched dismally at that weekend's offerings dancing in their tacky heels and necking back pints of lager. Is that the best that the night could offer? Not one of them was up to his standards. He had a particular type that he was attracted to, and he would not waste a moment on anyone that didn't fit the bill. He wanted someone that would make him look good, and there was currently no one worth splashing his cash on. Swigging back the last of his gin, Jake grabbed his jacket and headed into the coldness of the damp October night.

The streets were filled with drunken clubbers stuffing their faces with greasy offerings to calm their food cravings and soak up the alcohol from their bowels. The smell of fried food turned Jake's stomach as he wandered past the doorway of the Turkish kebab house. It was bursting at the seams with inebriated customers trying desperately to count their money as they swayed from side to side. He shuddered at the sight as he continued his walk. An elderly man held onto a shop window, trying to keep himself upright as he emptied the contents of his stomach onto the concrete floor. Jake zipped his jacket up around his mouth to try and deter the stench of vomit that had wafted towards him on the fresh autumnal breeze.

A Friday night alone was a bit of a rarity, as he hadn't had a weekend to himself in several years. If he wasn't in the UK with his newest bimbo draping herself around his neck or straddling his thighs during a night of passion, he was in another city in another country, with yet another gullible girl. Then he had met Katy. He had spotted her long slender legs and perfect figure from the corner of the exclusive members' only nightclub. After watching her writhe about for hours and becoming aroused by her hypnotic dancing, he had sent her table a bottle of Don Perignon Champagne. This had won her attention. After a few hours of the usual chatting and charming, he had managed to persuade her to join him for an impulsive weekend in Paris.

After several seemingly perfect years together, he was angry that he had wasted all his money and time on her. In return, he had received no respect, had been given the cold shoulder, and Katy had completely shut him out of her life. Did she not realise what she had lost? There were plenty of women out there that would give him the respect and commitment he deserved.

Jake reached the solace of the member's only nightclub. Flashing his gold membership card to the steroid filled bouncer's guarding the doorway, he wandered down towards the muffled noise below. The humidity of the club hit his face as he reached the bottom of the dark stairwell. Pushing the door open, he was greeted by the stench of sweaty bodies that were crammed onto the dance floor and bouncing about to the ear-deafening beats of that weeks guest DJ. The laser lights dazzled him for a moment as he searched for a small gap in the crowd and made his way to the bar.

Arrogantly, he pushed his way to the front of the queue, ignoring the other drinkers' objections. After attracting the attention of one of the barmaids, he asked to speak to the manager. After a short while, a skinny man in his late fifties approached accompanied by a gorilla-sized bodyguard in his early twenties. After being greeted like a long lost family member, Jake pressed a handful of £50 notes into the manager's palm as he shook his hand. Patting Jake on the

back, the manager whispered his requirements to the bodyguard. Jake had succeeding in getting what he wanted again.
A group of pretty young clubbers were ushered away by the bodyguard, and Jake was shown to his own private table. Thanking the manager and taking a seat on the plush red velvet seats, Jake smiled smugly to himself as he took off his jacket and placed it on the shelf behind his head. A busty waitress arrived with a smile and put an unopened bottle of gin and a tall glass filled with ice onto the table, all compliments of the house.

Pouring his drink, Jake scanned the club and admired a few of the young ladies who graced the dance floor in their exposing outfits, leaving little to the imagination. How times had changed, he thought as his mind rewound to his younger days clubbing in London. Tight-fitting clothes had always been around but going out in almost just your underwear was certainly not clubbing fashion back then. Since hitting his 30's, he had started to feel a little too old to frequent clubs as most people seemed in the late teens or early twenties. Yet their innocence meant that he could groom them quite easily. Flashing a little cash and his latest Rolex watch had the youngsters throwing their bodies at him. These girls were great to use to his advantage just to satisfy a night of lust, but there wasn't much of a chase, which was the part that he liked most. The harder they were to impress, the more of a thrill he got. It was almost like an addiction. The harder the chase, the sweeter the catch.

Sitting back against the softness of the chair, he took a sip of his drink and felt the coldness of the liquid trickle down his throat. Nodding his head along with the beat, Jake scanned the crowds for anyone who looked worthy of his time. He noted a few possibilities that appeared to be a little more appealing. After analysing all potential prey in more detail from his hunting seat, he found that they were too fat, too ugly or too chav looking. He almost gave up hope until he saw the perfect victim. He followed her as she danced her way through the crowds to join a group of girls that had sat on a table closer to the dance floor.

He voluptuous figure had swayed like a pendulum, and she snaked gracefully through the mosh pit of drug-fuelled ravers that filled the dance floor. Her classy black figure-hugging dress and thigh high boots were enough to send any hot-blooded male into an aroused frenzy. As she turned, her perfect wide smile gleamed white under the UV lights as long, dark straight hair framed her flawless features. He had his target. Next, all he needed to do was to get her attention. He continued to watch her movements for a while to be sure she was not with a partner. After being convinced that she was alone, he made his way to where she was standing, and the excitement of the chase began to surge through his veins.

Jake stood a safe distance, not to invade her space and creep her out as she chatted with her friends. He occasionally caught her eye as she sipped her drink playfully through a straw, flashing her an innocent smile when their eyes met. After a few moments, he wandered closer to make his first move. Raising his voice above the music, his cheesy chat-up line began.

"Hey, I hope you don't mind, but I need your advice!" he said, leaning into her ear so she could hear him.

"Sure, What's up?" she replied, eager to help.

"Let's say I saw an incredibly sexy person. Do I go up and talk to them, or is that too direct?" he continued.

"I think you should just go for it and go talk to them! Hope that helps?" she replied with a smile, turning back towards her friends.

"Okay, thanks for your time!" He paused for just a moment then, touching her arm to get her attention, he continued. "Hi, I'm Jake. I think your kind of sexy and thought that I should be direct..." he cringed at the corniness of his own words.

"That was good...but not good enough sorry, I am not interested!" she smiled, showing her perfect white teeth, then turned her back on him.

The rejection surged through his whole body. Her voice was soft and sultry as it sent a vibration of shivers down his spine. She was just perfect and he knew that he had to work a little harder to get what he set out for. It was time to go up a gear and start stage two of his pursuit.

Jake wandered to the bar and ordered a tray of mixed flavour gins to be sent to the girl's table. He wrote a note and passed it to the bartender, advising that it should only be given to the lady with the incredible smile whom he pointed out. The bartender took over the drinks and set them down on the table as the group firstly objected to the order. Then after a moment of confusion, the woman with the smile read the note confirming that they were compliments of an admirer who would cover their bill for the remainder of the evening. Then, they erupted in cheers as they all grabbed a glass and toasted the air in all directions to the anonymous sender.

The girl with the smile, however, asked the bartender whom the admirer was. After a giveaway glance and nod towards Jake, he knew his cover had been blown. But the oldest tactic he knew had worked as she wandered over to thank him. Introducing herself as Emily, she spent the remainder of the night in his company. Jake had then had a chance to really show his charismatic ways. Reeling her in after that had been as easy as pie. All he had to do was show interest in everything she was interested in, ask loads of questions about her and throw in lots of compliments.

She had been pretty hard to convince on accepting another date, but after softening her with his relationship sob story and plying her with numerous varieties of gin, Emily had reluctantly given Jake her number. He thanked her for her company, kissed her hand as a gentlemanly goodbye, paid the bill and left the club on a high, knowing that he had charmed her into wanting more. He had then sent her a text message thanking her for her company as he sat alone in his penthouse hotel suite. A few minutes later, Emily had replied, thanking him for his kindness and company. Securing a date with his next text for the following evening, Jake went to bed that night an accomplished man.

The next evening Jake had met Emily at an expensive restaurant in the city. She had arrived in a very elegant dress that hugged her desirable figure. Her radiant smile and large brown bambi-like eyes had turned almost every head in the room. After pulling out her chair to take a seat, Jake ordered a bottle of Chateau Le Pin and settled in the seat opposite her. The conversation had just flowed from that moment. Jake had asked her so many questions about herself and showed interest in everything she divulged. Then, on request, Jake impressed her with many fake stories he created about friends that didn't even exist. There hadn't been any awkward moments of silence between them as he showed interest in almost everything she had said. This was one of the easiest ways to get into the knickers of any woman. Listen attentively, ask the right questions, hear what they were saying and show compassion or interest in even the most boring stories.

After a successful second date, Emily had fallen victim to his charms, and as soon as they had found their way back to his hotel, she had thrown herself at him the moment the elevator started its ascent to his penthouse suite. The sex was out of this world. It was one of the most incredible nights he had spent with a complete stranger, apart from Katy and a few other women he had forgotten the names of. His predatory success had increased his libido, and he could have gone all night, high off his own ego.

This was the only time that he actually felt desirable. It was almost as if every woman he bedded gave him that female attention he had been starved of as a child. Those countless nights that he had laid in his bedroom, fearing the creaking sounds that he could hear from the expanse of his parent's stately home and hiding under the sheets from the darkness, wanting to feel the reassuring warmth of his mother's gentle touch. Wetting his bed through fear of walking the dark Victorian corridors just to use the toilet and then being punished for his tardiness at the mercy of his father's leather belt as his mother looked on expressionlessly.

This was when he started to resent his mother and females, in general. She should have been there to protect him and comfort

him, not allow him to feel pain. The visible scars that he wore covered his torso from these many physical attacks by his father were a constant reminder of his loveless childhood.
His father had demanded he be sent to boarding school to toughen him up. That had been at the tender age of just six. His clothes had been packed in a single suitcase. He had then been carried, kicking and screaming, then strapped into the rear of the car, regardless of his sobs and pleas. Then, after a few hours of travelling, he was abandoned to the strange isolation of an unfamiliar mansion on the other side of the country. He only saw his parents during holidays and, as he grew, had wished that he could have remained at school, where he received more attention from the staff than he did his own parents.

His mother was an expressionless and emotionless woman who showed no affection to anyone. She was very petite and said very little after years of being bullied and belittled by his father. She had pandered to his fathers every whim. She even turned a blind eye to his affairs that he didn't even try to conceal from her. Jake had stumbled upon many sordid scenes after another dinner party that his parents had thrown for their high society friends. Often finding his drunken father in between the legs of yet another inebriated young woman in full view of anyone unfortunate enough to wander in. He was sure his mother had witnessed his betrayal on several occasions.

It was almost as if she had been programmed to obey his father, accepting the way he behaved to live the lifestyle she had married into. This had made his mother cold and distant. Nothing surprised her, and nothing upset her. He had neither seen her cry or smile. Apart from once, when his father had fallen down the stairs and had stayed in a hospital in a back brace for a few weeks. This had allowed a faint smile to creep across her tightly pursed lips.

The house had been different for that time. He had actually felt a little warmth return to his mother's eyes, and she had even shown him a little kindness. He had been taken by surprise when she had offered him her awkward maternal embrace after he had fallen from a tree in the garden and sobbed his way into the usual cold void of their stately home. But that spark of affection soon disappeared as soon as his father had returned home, leaving Jake to feel rejected and unwanted again.

His father was an arrogant man. Born into the wealth of his ancestors, who had made their money in the coal trade. He had used his status to its full advantage. To the outside world, he was charismatic, funny and caring. He would do anything to help his friends or colleagues as this put them in his debt. He would put on the most outrageously opulent gatherings and was always the life and soul of the party, offering his guests the best of food and drink that his money could buy.

His less wealthy friends lapped around him like dogs as he offered them morsels of his lavish lifestyle. He was like their golden ticket to paradise. Yet, when the parties were over, and the house returned to its normal eerie silence, the falsely charming and funny man that had lit up the room with his laughter and smiles had regressed to a cold, selfish, controlling and unpredictable tyrant. He would erupt with violent outbursts the moment anything didn't go his way, sending Jake bolting for the safety of his bedroom to avoid falling victim to his father's rage again.

His mother had often sported a black eye or bruising to her slender arms, that she tried to conceal with her clothing. Even with his rage, infidelity and mood swings, she remained by his side like an obedient slave. After an argument, his father would return home with bunches of flowers, expensive gifts and whisk his mother away for a few days, leaving Jake alone to fend for himself.

Jake had never known what it was like to actually feel wanted. There had never been a moment in his childhood that he could remember that had brought him happiness except for a puppy he had been bought to keep him company through the school holidays. That had been the only thing that had ever shown him affection. He had trained the puppy to do everything at his command. The dog grew to be a loyal and obedient companion who remained by Jakes side wherever he went. He had lasted for twelve years, and the pain of the loss had ripped through Jakes heart. Yet his parents did not seem to care about his grief. He had been given even more money to distract him as a supplement to their time and affection.

He had learnt that money could get him anything he desired. He had always been a loner at school, but his wealth bought him friends who used him for free nights out, high society parties he threw when his parents were away at their villa in St Tropez or exclusive clubs he could buy his way into. People gave him recognition and respect when they saw his wealth and lavish lifestyle. He had been born Francis Jacob but had changed his name as soon as he was old enough to just Jake. He had hated his name, having been teased and bullied by the other boys at the boarding school, telling him it was a girl's name. Even at school, he had been a bit of a loner.

Jake had noticed that his wealth had its benefits, and he thrived on the attention he could buy from the women he met. These women gave him the affection that he didn't receive from his own flesh and blood. Money meant nothing to him, but it seemed to hypnotise others into doing anything he wanted. He could treat them as he felt fit, like the dirty sluts they were. The majority were no better than prostitutes, offering their bodies in return for his conditional generosity, time and attention.

Emily knew nothing of Jakes past. This meant he could tell her anything he pleased, and she naively accepted his every word. The more time Jake spent with her, the more he was sure that she was the most perfect woman for him to groom. She lapped up the attention he gave her with his displays of wealth. The expensive gifts and city breaks away made her a slave to his needs. It also made her someone that he could control, just as his father had his own mother. Jake became obsessed with Emily very quickly, and after an intense few months of love-bombing her with so many gifts and attention, he knew that he never wanted to let her go. He had also managed to steer her attention away from her friends. His attention had commandeered almost all of her time without her even being aware.

They spent every weekend together in a different city or a foreign country, enjoying the most refined foods and best hotel suites available. After a while, Jake had noticed that Emily no longer bubbled with excitement when he presented her with another outrageously expensive gift or surprised her with yet another self indulgent weekend away. The spark had started to disappear from her eyes just as he had witnessed in Katy. He didn't understand how his gifts failed to make her happy. Then after a fantastic meal at a top restaurant in Paris, Emily had blurted out that she wanted to spend more time with her friends. This had angered Jake, as he didn't see why she would rather be with them than him. Was she not grateful for everything he did for her? He had raged about her being selfish as what was he supposed to do if she was not with him? He would not lower himself to spend a night with her mates in a tacky "happy hour" pub, watching her get drunk and getting the attention of dirty old men that were just eager to get in her knickers. She should be spending every weekend with him and not acting as if she was single.

His harsh words had upset Emily, who had left the restaurant in a hurry and disappeared in the back of a taxi. He had been welcomed back at the hotel with complete silence. Even after his attempts to seduce her, he had fallen asleep enraged by her rejection. Waking up early, Jake had ordered a champagne breakfast and booked two tickets for her favourite band in Rome the following month. It had worked a treat, and this had set the pattern for their future arguments.

After a few further hiccups, he had agreed to her meeting with her friends on the understanding that he could be her taxi and that she didn't dress like a whore. Emily had initially objected to his demands as she didn't see what the issue was. He had always liked the way she had dressed and found it attractive. It was her body, and she could wear what she wanted. Jake had a different opinion. It was his body, not hers, and he would change her entire wardrobe if he had to.

Taking her to London, Jake spoilt her with a shopping spree for a new wardrobe. He felt a surge of pleasure as he dictated what she tried on. The more she obeyed, the more aroused he became, to the point that he could not control his urges anymore, and even after she had objected to his advances, Jake had taken what he deserved as payment for his gifts. He was becoming a carbon copy of his father.

Things were again running smoothly until Emily was made redundant and got a new job. From that moment, her nights and weekends were taken up with work. He hardly saw her, as she would go clubbing with her new friends straight from the office and stroll in as the sun rose. She had started to ignore his calls and text messages, making Jake convinced that she was having an affair. He had to come up with a plan to regain control of what was rightfully his. He had invested all his time and money on her, so the most he deserved was her loyalty and undivided attention.

Chapter 3

Too Good to be True

The office around Emily bustled with excitement as the end of the shift neared. Just another 5 minutes to wrap up her latest call, and she would be out with the usual gang, partying until sunrise. As she went through the familiar statements that now seemed to fall off her tongue robotically, she eagerly watched the minutes disappear on her screen. Saying her goodbyes to her final client of the day, she quickly logged herself off her system and placed her headset on the desk. Saturday nights were the best as there was no work to drag herself into the following morning, still stinking of the alcohol from the night before and often, still a little tipsy.

Taking her phone out of her bag, she noted at least seven missed calls from Jake and double the number of text messages. Didn't he get it? The more he begged her and demanded her time, the less likely she would want to spend it with him. She had been to his parent's home a few times that week to spend quality time together. But, on each occasion, his demands for attention, and constant need for reassurance, got too much for Emily to cope with. After just a few hours, she had retreated to the peaceful haven of her flat. She had started to find him too needy, and he was starting to suffocate her. Tonight was her night. She had explained this to him already. She had planned this night out with the girls in the office for the past few weeks. There had been a new club that they had all wanted to visit and had been given discount passes by the new manager that they had met in the pub during their lunch hour.

Jake had picked out that evening's outfit, which she had obediently placed in her backpack, just to keep the peace, placing it next to the concealed slinky dress she had planned to switch it for when she got to the club. She was not going out looking like a legal aid secretary. Taking her bag into the ladies' toilets, she stripped off and put on the hideous trouser suit that Jake had insisted she wore.

Ensuring that the buttons were done up to the neckline, not revealing too much of her cleavage. She reapplied her lipstick, undid the claw clip at the back of her head and tussled her long dark hair over her shoulders.

"So is that really what you wearing out with me tonight, missy?" said Tammy, one of her closest friends in the office, as she disapprovingly looked Emily up and down. "He has chosen it again, hasn't he! Didn't you stand up to him this time?"

"He chose it, but I will only be wearing it out of the building. I will be changing into this the minute we get into the club," Emily said, pulling out the little black number she had bought especially for the evening. "I refuse to wear this all night," said Emily, as her arms ran up and down her body. Wandering into a cubicle, she sat on the closed toilet seat and pulled on her thigh-high boots, concealing them as best she could underneath her trousers.

"He's a bit weird, you know, Jake. You could do so much better than him, Em. You shouldn't have to put up with this shit when you are old enough to make your own decisions. Christ, he acts like your father would have when you were a teenager out on your first date. Those legs and curves are to die for, and you need to let the world see them, not hide them away under the shapeless clothes he expects you to wear," Tammy stated.

"I know, Tam. It is driving me insane. He is totally obsessed with me. I know he will be hiding in his car, making sure that I am going where I said and with whom I told him. He will be watching to see that I am wearing what he approves of too. I am sick of it, but he just won't listen to my needs at all. It is always just about him!" Emily protested as Tammy wriggled into her Lycra bodysuit. "Damn, girl, you're hot!" she blurted out, as the material spread unforgiving over Tammy's perfectly toned yoga body.

Tammy smiled as she pulled on her red killer heels and touched up her make-up. "Joey is out tonight, and I am damn sure that I am making him mine by the end of the evening. If he doesn't want me after seeing me in this, I am sure that he is still exploring his own sexuality. LGBTQ and all that!" she announced, swinging her hips from side to side and simultaneously giving her finger a zig zag wag.

"I look like your innocent prudish friend, like Sandy in Grease!" Emily laughed as she grabbed Tammy's arm and headed towards the lift.

As they walked outside, Emily quickly scanned the street to see if she could see Jake's car parked anywhere. It didn't take too long for her to spot him. He was sat glaring at her as she kept her eyes fixed ahead. Nudging Tammy's ribs to acknowledge his presence, she hugged herself closer into the safety of her companion's arm. His behaviour made Emily feel nervous. She felt controlled in every aspect of her life and needed out, but had no clue how to deal with Jake. She was scared that he would become aggressive if she ended the relationship. She was unsure of his full capabilities and how far he would go just to keep her as his possession.

Eventually reaching the pub's haven, Emily flopped in relief into the plush red velvet seat as Tammy ordered their first drink. She felt her bag vibrate on her hip. Taking her mobile from the side pocket, she noted several texts from Jake since leaving the office. Opening the latest message, she began to read in disbelief.

"Why would you want to go out with someone that looks like they are out for a night working the streets, when we could have been in Prague this weekend. Don't lower yourself to her standard, your way better than the trash you are hanging out with. The outfit looks amazing on you. I can't wait to get you home! Call me. J X."

Emily didn't bother to reply. The anger burnt red on her cheeks. How dare he call her friend a whore! He had no clue about Tammy. Had he ever taken the time to meet her, he would have known that she was highly intelligent. She was currently studying law, and the call centre was her way of seeking financial independence from her family. Who was he to judge anyone when she had not ever seen him go to work to earn an honest living.

Tammy arrived back at the table and could see that something was bothering Emily.

"You OK Em?" she said in a concerned tone.

"He is totally unbelievable and out of order. I have just had a text from him the minute we walked through the door. Can't he just let me enjoy the night and give me some space?" Emily objected.

"Turn it off. You don't need it on anyway. All the guys will be here in the next hour, and we will already have drunk half the gin supplies in here. Don't let him get to you and try to enjoy the evening. Crash at mine tonight. He has no clue where I live, and anyway, he's not your keeper!" Tammy reminded her, taking a suck of her drink through her reusable chrome straw.

Emily agreed, turned off the phone and dropped it back in the side pocket of her bag. Picking up the ice-cold glass, she took a mouthful of the clear liquid and let out a sigh of pure pleasure. Tonight she was going to get wasted and push Jake from her thoughts. Tonight was about her and not him. At that moment, a few of the office crowd burst through the pub doors creating a Mexican wave volume of excitement as they descended on the poor barmaid.

"Let's get the party started then! Tequila shots all around!" shouted one of the girls, ordering an additional two for Emily and Tammy.

Emily then knew that she wasn't going to survive the morning without a killer hangover.

Emily's eyes tried hard to stay open. Her head pounded, and the room still spun. The settee's soft velour was wet with her dribble, and the seat cushions had almost ejected themselves from underneath her drunken body weight. Her neck ached from the position she had woken in. Thrusting her arms under her chest, she pushed herself upwards into a cobra style yoga pose before swinging her feet reluctantly to the ground.

Everything around her seemed to move. She felt her stomach tighten with panic as she tasted the acidic build-up in her throat and tried to stop herself from vomiting. Emily took a deep breath, closed her eyes and tried to keep her body upright. She swayed uncontrollably from side to side. It was almost as if the room had taken on the gentle current of the ocean. She gripped the edge of the settee to stop herself from falling back into its softness. She forced her eyes open and took in the surroundings. Scanning the room in confusion, Emily didn't recognise a thing. Where the hell was she, and who the hell was that?

She looked down to see a half-naked unidentified male lying on the floor at her feet. In a sudden grip of panic, Emily looked down to check that she was still fully clothed. Noting that she was still wearing the slinky little black dress that had risen around her waist, displaying her knickers that were still firmly in place, her fear subsided. The strange room was a mess. Empty bottles and cans lay strewn across the carpet and filled the glass coffee table that sat in the centre. The curtains were part closed, allowing the cruel sunbeams to penetrate into the aftermath of their drunken night. Emily's eyes squinted at the brightness as her blurry vision scanned the room for any further signs of life.

A sudden movement caught her eye from under a pile of jackets in the far corner, and the familiar jet black curls of Tammy escaped from beneath the makeshift blanket. Emily felt a surge of relief fill her body. She must have been at Tammy's flat. She had never been there, which is why nothing was familiar. Then Emily suddenly thought of Jake. Her stomach tightened again with fear. He would be furious that she had not contacted him. She needed to get home as she knew he would be checking up on her the first chance that he got.

Emily pushed herself to her feet, steadied herself against the arm of the settee and took her first few shaky steps. Navigating her way over the sprawled legs of the man below her, she recoiled at the sight of his bollocks hanging out of the side of his boxers. Blindly, she searched for her belongings and, after successfully locating her bag and thigh-high boots, she tiptoed out of the humid staleness of the room and into the freshness of the early morning breeze.

Emily sat on the step and pulled the crumpled suit out of her bag. She hoisted the trousers up over her waist and zipped them up around her dress. Then pulled the now crumpled shirt up over her shoulders and slipped on her office shoes. She looked almost presentable enough for a day at work if it hadn't have been for the black smudge of mascara that had rubbed onto the shirt collars as she hastily dressed in the cold morning air. Emily took out her phone from her bag, took a deep breath and paused before pressing the screen to life.

Dozens of notifications filled her home screen, the majority from Jake. She pinned in her passcode and ignored the text alerts that kept popping up on her screen as she tried to locate where the hell she was. It had been a while since she had woken up in a strange flat in an unknown location. As she desperately tried to find her whereabouts on her Google maps, an incoming call from Jake disrupted her search. She froze mid-breath as she stared at his picture on the phone screen and waited for what seemed a good few minutes until, eventually, her answerphone kicked, and his call was diverted. Emily relaxed and let out her held breath, then checked the time. It was only just after 7am and he was already checking up on her.

Shaking her head in frustration, she continued her search on Google maps and punched in her postcode to get the quickest route home. A brisk walk in the fresh air would do her good after the amount of alcohol she had consumed. Her breath stank, her feet were sore from dancing, and her neck ached from being passed out unconsciously on the settee. Emily couldn't wait to get home to the comfort of her bed. Noting it was just a twenty-minute walk to her flat, she popped in her earplugs and followed the dulcet tones of the male navigator on her mobile phone.

Reaching the welcoming sight of her flat, Emily hurried up the stairs, unlocked the door and unzipped her boots. Making a beeline for her bedroom, she threw the curtains closed to blackout the brightness of the returning sunshine. Stripping out of the layers of uncomfortable clothes, exposing just her underwear, she pulled back the covers and slid herself between the sheets. Placing her mobile on the bedside cabinet, she turned on her side and sunk into the comfort of her own bed. Within moments she was sound asleep.

Chapter 4

New Horizons

Jake was furious. He had been awake all night waiting to hear from Emily. He had told her to contact him so he could give her a lift back to the safety of her flat. Pressing his mobile against his ear, he tried her number again for the umpteenth time. Tapping his leg in agitation, Jake waited impatiently as the answerphone kicked in yet again. Slamming his mobile onto the plush cushion next to him in frustration, he picked up his coffee mug and looked down the length of the Orangery that covered the southwest side of his parents stately home. This is where he took his breakfast every day as it was calm and looked out over the acres of ornamental gardens that his father had spent tens of thousands having landscaped to mimic that of Blenheim Palace.

The morning sun had just started to penetrate the glass roof, and its rays teased through the vine leaves that clambered above him. Jake was distracted for a moment by the hazy beams that created kinetic patterns on the ceramic tiles beneath his feet, as the electric fan blew a gentle breeze through the room. He took pleasure from the first touch of warming rays that reached his face. Closing his eyes, Jake breathed in deeply to calm his anxious mind. After a few minutes of enjoying the morning's serenity, he checked his watch. It was now 7am, and he still had no clue where Emily was or even if she was OK. How dare she go out and just not bother to answer his calls or even have the respect to send a text to calm his growing concerns. Did she not know how much he cared about her?

His cheeks reddened with anger as he jumped to the conclusion that she must have hooked up with someone else during the night and spent the night with them. That's what happens when you go out with trash for friends. You end up acting like them, he thought. He had to regain some kind of control otherwise, Emily would just slip through his fingers as Katy had. But how was he going to do this when she spent every day at work and most weekends with her new friends. He hardly saw her now that she had a new social life. She had changed so much since meeting Tammy, and he didn't like it, he wanted his old Emily back. The Emily that had once given him all her time and attention. He needed to get rid of her new friends, but how was that even possible since she saw them every day at work? Then an idea came into his mind.

It was after 3pm when Emily was eventually woken by the impatience of her hungry cat, Jasper, tapping the side of her face. Initially, she felt confused by her surroundings but, after allowing herself to come around, she pushed herself up from her bed, grabbed her dressing gown and stumbled her way to the kitchen with the cat meowing loudly at her feet. Recoiling from the smell, Emily emptied the contents of the cat food tin into a bowl and placed it under the nose of her feline flatmate, letting out a sigh of relief from the noise that banged about inside her mind. Flicking on the kettle, she wandered across the room and threw open the French doors to allow in some fresh air to help to un-fog her mind. She felt dreadful and could hardly remember getting back to the flat that morning. Taking a mug from the kitchen cupboard, she made herself a coffee and wandered to the balcony.

Taking a seat on the small Mexican tiled bistro style chair, Emily threw her head back against the glass door and welcomed the afternoon sun-rays on her face. The sounds of children playing in the park opposite filled her fuzzy mind. She could quite easily have fallen back to sleep in the sun but needed to remain awake so that she could deal with Jake if he arrived unannounced. Finishing off the warm drink, she felt her stomach rumble and made her way back inside to make some boiled eggs to pacify her hunger. As they bubbled away in the pan, Emily wandered into her bedroom to retrieve her mobile phone. Way too many missed calls and messages from Jake filled her home screen. She knew she had to contact him but really couldn't deal with any confrontation at that moment as her head still pounded away from the vast amounts of alcohol she had consumed.

Checking her social media, she smiled at the photographs that Tammy had shared of their crazy previous night out. It shed a lot of light on why she felt as rough as she was and why she was still so tired that she could have slept on a chickens lip. Taking the eggs from the pan, she grabbed the loaf of bread and wandered back outside into the warmth of the early spring afternoon. It was so lovely to enjoy the return of warm blue skies after a long cold winter. How she could do with a week of lazing about in the hot Greek sunshine topping up a tan, eating gyros and drinking ouzo, she thought. But with her change in finances, there was no way she could afford a holiday that coming year. Her new income just covered her rent and bills with little to spare to contemplate saving. The thought of money caused a tightening in her throat. She daren't even think about how much she had spent on her night out with Tammy.

Flicking onto her mobile banking app, she punched in her passcode and waited anxiously for her balance to populate on the screen. Seeing the minus figure in bold black writing caused her heart rate to increase as panic set in as she wondered how on earth she was going to make this month's rent. She had another three weeks before payday, and the rent was due in just a week. She had never missed a payment to her landlord. Come to think about it, she hadn't been overdrawn in years. Emily scanned the outgoings of her account and noted a £150 cash withdrawal from the previous night. How did anyone spend that amount of money on a night out? She must have some cash left in her bag, she thought, as she stood up and rushed to check her purse.

Emptying the small change into her hand, she flopped in dismay over the arm of the settee and onto the soft seat pads that caught her fall. She had to do something to get some extra cash. A second job possibly. Early morning cleaner or paper round, if that was still a thing. Jasper jumped up onto her stomach and padded his paws into the softness of her dressing gown, and started to purr loudly. Giving his face a gentle rub, Emily checked her email account to see if she could distract her mind with anything of interest. The money would have to wait until tomorrow when she could actually think straight and develop some plan of action.

Just as she was about to put her phone down to run a bath, Jake's number appeared on the phone. Hesitating again for a second, Emily reluctantly answered his call to face his wrath.

"Em? Em? Are you OK? Where the hell have you been? Do you know I haven't slept a wink waiting for you to call? I thought you were hurt or something bad had happened to you. How dare you do that to me after everything I do for you! If you have to ignore my calls, then at least answer my texts and give me some respect. So what the hell happened last night?" burst Jakes angry voice through the device.

"Don't shout, OK! My head hurts, and I am really not up for an argument. I stayed at Tammy's last night as we got completely wasted, and I have no clue how we even got there. I don't even think I checked my phone and wouldn't have heard your calls over the loud music. Give me a break, J!" Emily replied.

"You stayed at Tammy's? So you didn't find time to let me know you were safe. So who the hell did you go there with? I bet you were with someone else, weren't you? Did he do it for you? Was he good? Was he worth it?" Jake said accusingly. "You bring this on yourself, Em, by being the way you are! It's you who make's me angry and react the way I do! If you just messaged me or answered my calls, then I wouldn't think the way I do!' he bluntly stated, passing full responsibility to her.

"Is that really what you think? Is that all you care about? Do you really think I would be unfaithful? I was there with Tammy and her flatmate. I slept on the settee and woke up fully dressed with a cricked neck, if you must know! Do you remember what it's like to go out with friends and have a good time, huh? Maybe you should get some mates of your own and go out with them instead of relying on me for your social life. Just leave it, Jake, and just leave me alone. I don't need any of this today. I have other worries to deal with!" and with that, she hung up and turned off her phone.

Emily's face had reddened in anger at his accusations. How dare he! How dare he think she had little respect for herself! She pushed a disgruntled Jasper to the floor, and wandered to the bathroom, pushed the plug into the bath and turned on the hot water tap. This is where she did her thinking and relaxed from anything that caused her to worry. Taking the Lavender bath salts out of the cupboard, she emptied the remaining contents into the bath and watched as the crystals melted in the heat of the water. Placing her foot over the tub, she dipped her toe in carefully to check the temperature. Dropping her dressing gown onto the floor and lifting her bed shirt over her head, Emily stepped into its welcoming warmth.

She dipped her shoulders beneath the surface and leaned her head back over the roll-top of the bath. Her mind wandered to her heated exchange with Jake. Was it really her fault? Had she acted as disrespectfully as he suggested? Maybe she was out of order, and if she had just let him know where she had been, things would have been okay between them. But she hadn't really done anything wrong? It had been her night out and her choice where she had stayed. It wasn't as if she had told Jake she would need a lift. She had actually said to him that she would call if she had any problem getting home. It wasn't as if they lived together, so he wasn't waiting for her to get in. And anyway, he should trust her! She had never once given him any reason not to!

She plunged her head beneath the water briefly and reached for the coconut shampoo. Pouring some of the silky liquid into her hands, she rubbed it into a lather on her hair. The aroma transported her in an instant to warmer distant lands deep in her memories. A time when she had had no worries to deal with. Those hot relentless days under the unforgiving Greek August sunshine, as she worked up a sweat harvesting figs.

Siestas curled up under the shade of an olive tree next to Tom after a hard morning's graft. Juicy Greek Salad dripping in olive oil, melt in the mouth feta cheese and the homely aroma of yeasty freshly baked bread, all spread out on a towel as they drank red wine and sat on pure white limestone pebbles. Wrapped in each others arms, watching the perfect blue hues of the ocean as they had lapped up the last of the sunrays. Then the hypnotic displays of the golden hour as the sun sank into the horizon, spewing an apocalyptic palate of magnificent splendour across the darkening skies. How they had watched the moonlight dancing over the blackened sea as the cicadas chirped away in the wild thyme and sage that filled her lungs with their intoxicating aroma. Those times with Tom had been so memorable, and part of her had wished she had never left.

Jake was livid. How dare she hang up on him without as much as an apology for her behaviour. He felt his face redden, and the vein in his forehead pulsate as his heart rate rose uncontrollably. He wanted to go around to her flat that instant and confront her. Show her how angry she had actually made him feel. He paced the kitchen as his mind tried to focus on regaining control as the anger surged through his body. He had to release his frustration somehow as it was becoming too much to bare. Picking up the metal stool from under the breakfast bar, Jake hurled it as hard as he could across the room. It bounced over the kitchen counter, knocking off everything in its path, sending pots and pans crashing to the floor as shards of wine glasses exploded on the ceramic tiles. The stool finally came to rest in the butler sink after taking a chunk out of the wooden worktop.

Jake felt a moments calm from his outburst. He didn't really care about the destruction he had caused. He didn't even try to hide the evidence. The maid would clean up the mess anyway. That's what she was paid to do. He turned his back on the carnage, calmly picked up his mobile from the kitchen counter and headed into the study as if he had done nothing wrong.

Having spent an hour in the warmness of her bath and in the company of fond memories, Emily dried herself off. Wandering back into the quietness of the living room, she took out her laptop from its bag at the side of the settee. Placing it on the coffee table, she sat on the soft shag pile of the rug and set about searching for some old photographs of happier times in Greece. She hadn't thought about Tom for such a long time and wondered where he was at that moment. Her memories had ignited a desire to see just how happy and carefree she had once been.

She pressed the "power on" button of the laptop and waited patiently. Punching in the letters of her password, the home screen burst to life with all her usual documents and files filling the crystal clear blue sea screen saver in the background. Finding the photograph file, she oozed over the happy memories that filled her screen.

A notification popped up on Emily's laptop, altering her that she had received a new Email. Checking her mail, she was taken straight to her Linked In profile inbox. Opening the message, Emily started to read.

"Dear Miss White,

We have been approached by a highly reputable broadcasting company looking to recruit an experienced voice-over artist. They have selected your voice as a potential candidate. Your role would involve providing voice-over recordings for national campaigns within the TV industry, working alongside some high profile clients.

Please advise us if this position would be of interest to you so we can submit your application.

Kindest Regards

Ms. R Emery
Recruitment officer
Voloquent "

Emily was gobsmacked. She had worked with Voloquent on several occasions in the past. This would bring in a substantial income, depending on the complexity of the role. It was a perfect solution to her financial situation, and if possible, she could work around her current work commitments. She didn't need any time to consider the offer. Hitting the reply button, she sent her acceptance for them to submit her application. Emily felt an instant weight lift from her shoulders and walked to the cupboard to get a wine glass. One drink to celebrate wouldn't do her hangover any harm, she thought.

Chapter 5

Life isn't Perfect!

It had been a few days since she had sent her reply to Voloquent. As yet, she had not received any response from her interest in the job advertised. She knew that it could take weeks before she heard back from them, but she was craving to get back into the studio and earn some decent cash. She had even found herself flicking through the holiday websites looking for a perfect week away in the sun and dreaming of cocktails as she lazed about doing nothing day after day.

She had also not seen or heard from Jake since their argument, which also worried her. He was always so needy of her time and attention that his quietness was so out of character. Deciding to let her stubbornness go and be an adult about things, Emily planned to pay him a visit after work instead of heading to the pub to meet Tammy. Maybe she did need to spend more time with Jake, she thought as her stomach became anxious about his lack of contact. Taking her last call of the day, she headed straight to the stairs ahead of Tammy, whom she knew would try and talk her out of weakening and backing down.

It almost took her an hour to reach the Surrey countryside's leafy suburbs after the madness of navigating the city rush hour. Finally, she saw the looming dark concrete pillars and black ornate cast-iron gates that concealed the imposing stately home from view. Emily slowed down as she approached the driveway. The automatic gates swung open, and she made her way down the sweeping tree-lined driveway passing by acres of perfectly mowed lawns, before eventually reaching the front of the yellowing greyness of the sprawling mansion.

The house was far to Gothic for her liking. Gargoyles and arched windows with mullioned glazing loomed above her like a million eyes watching almost every move she made as she stepped out of the car. The eerie sensation the house omitted, always made her feel nervous as she expected to see ghostly apparitions staring back at her from the many darkened windows that overlooked the driveway. Quickly making her way across the gravel driveway, Emily walked towards the sizeable dark oak-panelled front door and up the steps that had been smoothed into dips by centuries of footfall. Pressing the intercom on the door pillar, Emily waited patiently for a response. After about five minutes, a voice crackled through the shiny silver box.

"Can I 'elp you?" came the shaky Cockney tones of an aging Isobel, who had worked for the family for decades.

"Hi Isobel, I am here to see Jake if he is at home?" Emily responded with a smile.

"Give me a few minutes to check 'an I'll get back to you!" and with that, the box fell silent.

Emily turned to look at the gardens as she waited for the returning voice. Tall pine and oak trees lined the driveway back towards the entrance gate, while smaller flowering bushes had been pruned to perfection between each trunk. The grass to each side of the drive had been cut in stripes that mimicked a bowling green. She was sure that they must have measured each blade to check they were uniformed in size, as it was impossible to get anything that precise. The sky above was heavy with dark grey clouds and looked to threaten rain. Emily shuddered as a sudden cold wind blew across her bare legs and lifted her skirt. She hugged her cardigan into her chest and wished that Isobel would hurry before the rain came. Jake had told her so many times that he thought she was losing her marbles and was getting quite forgetful. Emily hoped that Isobel hadn't forgotten that she was waiting at the door.

As if by magic, the oak panelled door creaked open and Isobel's cheery wrinkled face popped around the door.

"Jake is in the orangery. Do you remember how to get there?" Isobel enquired.

"I think I will be fine, Isobel," Emily nodded in response.

And with that, Isobel turned and hobbled through the adjoining doorway then disappeared from view.

Emily stood for a second and took in the grandeur of the hallway. The red-carpeted concrete staircase curved its way above her to either side and was guided by the most decorative dark oak handrail she had ever seen. The ceramic floors tiles beneath her feet formed three-dimensional white, grey, black and sandstone cubes that made her feel quite dizzy as she stared ahead. A vast dimly lit golden lantern, hung from the vaulted ceiling above her, providing a little light from the darkness of the day. The walls were papered a deep maroon red above a waist-high oak panel that surrounded the hallway. A massive portrait of a portly old gentleman wearing hunting attire and sporting a horse-riding hat hung imposingly on the wall in front of her. The house smelt musty like a museum and felt empty of any homely warmth from its sheer size.

She made her way through numerous oak panelled rooms decorated with opulent wallpapers and gold-framed portraits of forgotten ancestors. Forlorn antique furniture had been discarded into unused rooms, just to fill their void and gave not comfort, but a sad eeriness to their presence. She counted several discarded Chesterfield chairs, pushed into corners, hugging unlit fireplaces or vacantly looking out over the acres of empty lawns. The whole house was oppressive and creepy until she reached the light airiness of the Victorian Orangery. This was situated to the back of the property and where she found Jake sat on the cane conservatory settee.

"Jake? I haven't heard from you for days and was worried about you. Is everything OK?" Emily questioned in concern for his unusual behaviour.

"I have thought that maybe you needed a little bit of distance from me and that I might have been suffocating you a little too much with my constant texts and calls. I wanted you to know that I really don't mind if you have a little bit of your own space. I was out of order the last time we spoke, and I apologise for my behaviour," Jake replied as he stood up to approach Emily.

Opening his arms for an apologetic embrace, he continued, "I am sorry if I act a little insecure sometimes, but I know that I am so lucky to have such a beautiful woman in my life. I fear someone else will steal your heart from me. The thought makes me so scared and jealous. I know I have to stop being that way, so I have been working on my own issues the past few days!" he announced. "I decided you are right. I do need to catch up with old friends and get my own social life back. So, I have been chatting with a few of them online, and we are organising a night out for the end of the month!"

Emily was taken aback by his sudden apology. Jake never apologised as he believed he was never wrong. He would usually present her with a gift instead. She smiled at his acknowledgment that he was a little too dependent on her for everything and allowed him to pull her into his open arms. This was precisely what she had wanted him to accept for such a long time now. She was so glad that he actually could understand how unhealthy it was for them to be together constantly. She walked into his embrace and burrowed her head into the warmth of his chest, inhaling the familiar deep woody scent of his aftershave. She had missed him over the past few days, and the thought that he might have actually done something stupid had made her realise that she did have feelings for him, which were not so easy to walk away from.

This was the Jake that she longed for. The Jake that owned up to his faults and took responsibility for his ways. If he could stay this way, then their relationship could be so perfect. She did love him and knew that his behaviour was meant with good intentions. He just cared about her deeply and didn't want anything to happen to her. This was worth holding onto. After a few moments of silence, Emily pushed herself out of the clutch of his embrace and looked into his deep brown eyes.

"Jake, you know I love you and really am not interested in any other man. I would never ruin what we have or be unfaithful to you. Our relationship means the world to me, and I really appreciate that you care for me deeply too. I am sorry that I didn't text you or call you back to know I was OK with Tammy. It was selfish of me, and it won't happen again, I promise," Emily said sincerely.

"Apology accepted!" he said, pulling her into his welcoming lips. "So, what's been happening with you? Any news?"

"Well, actually, I have been headhunted for a job back in the studio, which would be incredible as it could support my current income and free my finances a little. Things are a little tight since I was made redundant, and it would be great to have some extra cash!" she announced.

"That's amazing, Em! So when do you start?" Jake inquired.

"I am still waiting to hear back from them, but it's only been a few days, so I guess they are still receiving applications and going through the ropes. It generally takes a little while for them to sort through the voices they chose before they agree on the right one for the role. I just wish they would hurry up and come to a decision as I am so ready to get back in the studio," Emily replied, pulling backward and away from Jakes arms.

Emily walked over to the long windows that looked out over the perfect gardens and watched as a few rabbits happily grazed on the luscious lawns. The evening sunshine had now broken through the dark clouds. Emily could feel its warmth on her face from the beams that reached her through the glass roof above.

"It is so peaceful here, Jake. You don't know how lucky you are having all of this just on a plate for you. You don't have to worry about money, a career or your future as this is destined to be yours. I can't even consider saving to afford a mortgage with the high rents that I have to pay. I am stuck in this cycle for a while to come, unless I win the lottery!" she said as she daydreamed through the glass.

"It's not all it looks, Em. This house is a huge burden that I have to bear for the sake of my ancestors. I feel obliged to take it on and to keep it in the family for the next generation. It's easy to think that I am lucky to have all this, but in reality, it's not as perfect as you think. There are so many areas of the house that have not been used for decades. Forgotten rooms filled with years of undisturbed dust and antique furniture that hasn't seen an arse for centuries. It is really a waste," he stated. "The house would be better as a hotel. At least then it would make money instead of being a money pit. The upkeep alone is several thousand a month, and then there are structural issues and damp that needs addressing. These houses were made for several generations to live in at once and not just three people. Plus, who knows, this could be yours one day too, and we could have little Jakes and Emily's running through these silent corridors creating life in this old tomb. That's all I really want, Emily, to love and care for you and to have a family of our own, " he said with so much honesty to his voice.

Emily turned back to look into the room and was greeted by a smiling Jake, who was sat on the arm of the cane settee. This was the first time he had ever suggested that they would live together and potentially have a family. The thought warmed through her as she considered what it would be like to be lady of the manor. Taking afternoon tea under the shade of the large oaks that skirted the ornamental gardens while their children played on the perfectly tendered lawns. It was almost as if the controlling, demanding, and selfish Jake had diminished, and a new, softer, more vulnerable version stood in front of her. He sounded so sincere in his words and spoke in a way she had never heard before. Emily walked towards Jake and pushed herself between his legs as he sat, then, pulling him forwards, she hugged him into her chest.

"This is all I want to Jake. I don't want us to fight or suffocate each other. I want us to get along and understand what we both want from each other. I had no idea that you felt the way you did, and maybe I have taken you for granted. I will be more considerate in the future," she promised.

"Me to Em, I will back off and give you more space," Jake responded. "Now, how about some food? I am starving!"

Chapter 6

The Plot Thickens

Emily stared at the email on her laptop in disbelief. Her heart raced in her chest, and she could feel the excitement build up in her throat as it burst uncontrollably out of her mouth,

"Yyyeeeesssss!!!! Oh, my God! I can't believe it! This is just amazing!" she said out loud, then reached for her mobile.

Dialling Jakes number, she read through the details of the email quickly so that she could fill him in on her good news, as she waited to hear his voice.

"Hey, baby? I was just thinking about you! How did you sleep? I miss our morning cuddles," Jake said in a sleepy morning voice.

"I got the job!! I only went and got the job didn't I!" she blurted out, without even hearing anything Jake had said. "Three weeks I have waited for a reply and thought I hadn't got it as I had not heard anything! This is amazing and a huge relief for my bank balance."

"That's amazing, Em! I knew you would get it! Your voice is just the best I know, but then I am a bit biased," he chuckled. "So a celebration it is then! Shall I come to yours and cook us up a meal, or shall we eat out at that new steakhouse in town, you know, the one you mentioned the other day?"

"Let's go out! I could do with a treat. It has been a while since we last went out. It's been great having the nights in and all, but tonight's a special occasion. I am back in the land of fame and fortune!" exclaimed Emily.

"I will book us a table and pick you up around 7pm. See you later!" and with that, Jake was gone.

Emily read through the email again more thoroughly. Happy with the employment offer and the agency's pay scale, she sent her acceptance then flopped back on the settee feeling accomplished. She couldn't believe that she was actually getting things back on track. Jake had backed off, giving her space to breath and had been really understanding of her needs for a few weeks now. She felt that they had reached a different stage of their relationship. Her work and social life were going really well, and now this. She loved everything about her life at that moment.

Looking around the room, she noted Jasper curled up in the afternoon sunshine on the faux fur grey rug next to the French doors. The sun was spilling in through the trees that lined the pavement in front of the flat. This had been the first Saturday that she had not had a hangover in a while, and she wasn't going to waste it. Pushing herself up from the comfort of her mustard velour settee, Emily wandered to the door and picked up her cardigan from the coat hook. Slipping on her comfy flats, she opened the door, headed down the stairs, onto the pavement and across the street to the welcoming lush green of the park.

The afternoon sun was warm, and the park was filled with families enjoying the summer's day. A small child wearing a blue helmet rushed past her on their red scooter, at an alarming speed for their size, with a frantic mother yelling from behind to "watch out for the nice lady!" The child, looking back confused by their mother's warning, thrust their foot to the ground in panic, sending them into an uncontrollable wobble and straight over the handlebars. Letting out an immediate scream, the concerned mother dashed to the side of her hysterical child and, hugging them close, brushed off the gravel from the graze on the palm of their child's hand. Emily smiled softly as she passed by and continued the walk around the park.

A variety of flowers filled the well-tended planters and flower beds that skirted the pathway to her right, creating a carpet of bright colours before her. The light breeze sent wafts of refreshing floral scents that filled her lungs as she strolled past their colourful displays. Beyond the flowers, a few groups of people sat on the recently mowed grass, enjoying a picnic in the peacefulness of the day, while a few older lads played football further in the distance. Emily took a seat on one of the benches that dotted the walkway to her left and watched as a squirrel rushed across the path and scurried up the trunk of the neighbouring tree. Everything felt so clear without her usual hangover haze. Emily closed her eyes and let the summer sunshine warm her face.

A gentle buzzing vibration brought her out of the serenity of the moment. Taking her mobile out of her cardigan pocket, she punched in her passcode and opened the Email notification. There in her inbox was an email from Voloquent confirming that her acceptance had been acknowledged, and they would advise her on her first studio session in due course.

Emily needed to share her excitement with someone. Tapping on Tammy's number, she sent her a message.

"Got some news! Fancy a Cuppa?"

Within a few seconds, she had her response, "Sure! Bring milk! ☺ "

Pushing herself off the bench, Emily started her walk to the other side of town.

As she arrived at the house, Emily was greeted at the door by Tammy's housemate, who still stank of stale alcohol. Remember the state he had been in the last time she had set eyes on him, Emily's face must have displayed her disgust.

"Hey Em, You will stay that way if the wind blows!" he suggested. "Tammy is in the living room catching up on her weekly soaps. Disturb her at your own peril!" he said, moving to one side, allowing her to pass through the overpowering pungency of his unwashed body odour. Emily scrunched up her face uncontrollably as she received another unpleasant waft as the door closed, sending a fresh wave in her direction.

Stepping over the pile of shoe's that lay discarded at the base of the staircase, Emily followed the dimly lit narrow magnolia corridor, to the rear of the property. Pushing the living room door open, Emily found a disheveled looking Tammy wrapped in her dressing gown and curled up on the settee, totally engrossed in the TV.

"You are looking a bit rough! Heavy night last night?" Emily questioned as she sat on the opposite side of the settee.

"You missed a blinder of a night, Em! That new club at the end of the high street was doing free shots with every drink, and you know how it is! Lost count after about six, but my body is really feeling it today!" Tammy responded as she put the TV on pause. "So what's your news? You aren't pregnant, are you? No! Don't answer. First, let me make a coffee, then you can tell me all about it!" and with that, Tammy disappeared into the kitchen.

Emily looked around the bleakness of the living room. There wasn't an area of the room that wasn't pilled high with forgotten clothes, crushed cans or empty snack packets. Every piece of furniture had been purpose bought to fill a student living accommodation. It was not homely at all, more like a doss house. The retro coffee table would have been more at home in her grandmother's house, along with the sideboard and TV unit. The settee and armchair both sagged with age, and ethnic throws covered the stained cushions beneath.

The curtains, hanging on the very few hooks remaining, were pulled closed, keeping out any reminders that it was actually daytime beyond. A dated floor lamp, with a floral fabric shade, threw a little pointless light across the far corner of the room. Remains of empty beer bottles and the previous night's takeaway lay discarded on the table. A large bluebottle fly buzzed about excitedly as it made the most of the forgotten leftovers.

Emily could not understand how anyone could have actually been happy living amongst the mess surrounding her. She had endured housework in the most terrible hangover states, just so that she could flop on the settee without any reminders filling the room and churning her stomach. Even with the mess surrounding her, she didn't judge her friend. Tammy's life consisted of intense periods of studying, working random shifts to pay her way and partying hard to let out her frustrations, to the point that Emily didn't really know when her friend actually found the time to sleep.

Tammy pushed her way back through the door using her foot, with the steaming mugs on a tray accompanied by a plate of stocked custard creams. Pushing aside the remains of the takeaway, she placed the tray shakily down on the coffee table, spilling some of their contents. Grabbing one of the biscuits and her mug that dripped on her bare knee from the spillage, she dunked the custard cream into the hot liquid and popped it in her mouth whole.

"So....What's the news?" Tammy said showering Emily with a few spluttered cumbs.

"I am not pregnant, so don't even think that! I got the job! The one I told you about. The advert with a famous actor, still to be disclosed!" Emily smiled.

"For real? That's so cool! So I am friends with someone almost famous even though no one will ever see your face!" Tammy mocked.

"It's the best kind of famous!" Emily responded with a smile. "All the money and no hassle."

"So when do you start? Are you giving up at the call centre? Where is it based? Will you meet anyone famous?" Tammy threw the questions at Emily like an excited child.

"No idea about anything just yet. I have to wait to hear from the company about my expected start date, but I hope not to finish at the call centre. I love it there!" Emily reassured.

"What does Jake think about it all? How will he cope if you are working two jobs? He already hates you not spending time with him!" enquired Tammy.

"He has actually been pretty good for the past few weeks Tam. It's almost as if he has matured a bit and changed his ways. He doesn't suffocate me with his demands for attention or my time. In actual fact, I haven't seen him or heard from him for a few days until I rang him this morning!" she said, in his defence. "He has chilled out quite a bit. I even got to choose my own clothes the last time we went clubbing, and he didn't bother me the whole time we were out!"

"That's what would bother me, though. How can he change so quickly from being totally controlling and obsessed to be the complete opposite? Something is not right, I am telling you. A snake can shed his skin, but he is still a snake, as my mamma always says!" Tammy said in her usual suspicious way.

"You are just looking for things. We had a good chat, and Jake understands my needs, and I also took on board how I had been taking him for granted. Anyway, I shouldn't have been acting like I was single and staying out all night. He is my boyfriend, and I should be telling him that I am OK and not dressing in a way that puts me in danger!" she protested. "I wanted to suggest that we go away on a girls-only holiday, my treat when I get my first paycheck. As long as we can get time off work and you can take a break from your studying! "

"Now that's an offer I can't refuse! I could do with getting some sunshine. I am almost pasty enough to join the Adams family on tour!" Tammy smiled, poking at her pale leg that was crossed underneath her. "So where shall we go?" she continued and taking her mobile from her dressing gown pocket.

Having spent over an hour at Tammy's, flicking through different holiday destinations and having decided on one of the Greek islands as their chosen holiday destination, Emily headed home. Quickly jumping in the shower, she washed, dried and applied her makeup. Happy with the result's she scrunched her hair and left it to dry naturally while she pulled out a few outfits to choose from.

She slipped on a little black figure-hugging dress, pulled up some stockings and admired her reflection in the mirror. It had been a while since she had gotten dressed up to go out with Jake, and she wanted to make him proud to be seen with her. He had always complimented her on how she had looked in this dress.

A knock on the door announced Jake's arrival. Grabbing her bag and slipping on her black heels, she rushed to open the door. Jake was stood entirely still and hiding his face with a dozen red roses. Pulling them downwards, his face emerged with a huge smile beaming from ear to ear.

"These are for you, my incredibly talented, beautiful girlfriend!" he said, as thrust the flowers into her arms. Leaning forward, Jake pulled her into his lips. "You smell divine!" he whispered as he pulled away. "So, are we good to go?"

"Yep! I have everything. I will just pop these in a vase, and we can head off" Emily smiled, turning to head into the kitchen.

"Is that what you are wearing?" questioned Jake as she walked away.

Emily turned to look back at Jake, who was looking her up and down. "Why wouldn't I? I look okay, don't I?" Emily questioned as she looked down at her dress.

"I guess if we were going to a tacky nightclub, but for The Savoy, maybe it's a little too, how do I say it.....cheap!" Jake said, so matter of fact.

"I beg your pardon? This is a designer dress that cost a fortune! In actual fact, you paid for it, and I have worn it on numerous dates out with you. You have always told me it's your favourite. Why change now? Why would you make me feel this way after the good day I have had?" She said, with confusion displayed all over her face.

"Maybe you have put on a little weight, or maybe it's the "time of the month" that makes it look that way and that is why you are getting so emotional about it. I don't know, but I would rather you change before we go, " shrugged Jake, as his words pierced Emily's heart.

Emily could feel herself welling up as anger boiled through her veins. Her cheeks began to burn red, and tears trickled down her face.

"GET OUT!! Just GET OUT!! I can't believe that you would be so horrible. I knew this was all a façade. I knew you couldn't keep it up, Jake. Why do you have to make me feel like shit when something good has actually happened to me!" Emily responded as she turned towards Jake, pushing him back towards the door.

Having successfully pushed him into the corridor outside, Emily slammed the door shut on his face and sank to the floor. She burst into tears at his hurtful words as Jake pounded the door, demanding that she open it. Today she had been on top of the world, thinking that everything was going perfectly, then Jake had swept the carpet from under her feet, and she felt so worthless yet again. How could he think it was okay to hurt her feeling like that?

Having been sat on the floor for almost twenty minutes while Jake persistently continued to apologetically beg and plead with her to let him in. Then, after getting no response, Emily could hear the anger and frustration emerge from him. He began punching and kicking the door, gradually getting harder and harder. Then he started a tirade of name-calling, insults and belittling. How could he change so dramatically? One minute he was so attentive and caring, and the next minute just so horrible. Emily's back bounced away from the door with each blow. Her heart raced in fear inside her chest, and tears rushed down her face, smudging her mascara. What if he broke the door down? What if he got in? Then, suddenly, his shouts and bangs stopped, and there was silence.

Emily remained sitting still, too scared to move or make a noise, just in case he was still out there. With tears still rolling down her cheeks, she fought back the sobs, remaining frozen to the spot on the floor. After staying still for enough time to be convinced he was gone, Emily rolled onto her knees and crawled as quietly as she could to the safety of the kitchen. This was the first time that Jake had actually scared her to the point that she had been terrified. A text message from Jake burst through on her phone.

"Don't think this is the end of this, Emily. Why do you have to make me so angry? If you had just done as I had told you, then we would be enjoying a meal right now. This is all your fault."

Maybe Tammy was right. Perhaps she did need to finally end things with Jake.

Chapter 7

Studio Time

Emily sat patiently on the black faux leather squeakiness of the retro egg chair and looked around to pass the time. The modern chic décor and ambient lighting of the waiting room made it feel luxurious compared to some of the studios that she had recorded at. A few aged music magazines scattered the contemporary coffee table, and a fern plant graced the table next to her chair.

Emily pulled out the script from a folder in her bag and started to read through its content, reminding herself of the exact way that they had expected her to deliver her voice. A sultry female peanut was the precise details of the role of a well-known chocolate brand. She had no clue who the famous actor was that would appear in the advert. This was something that she rarely found out until after recording her part to stop it from affecting her own performance. After a while, the receptionist called her name and escorted Emily through the corridors to the recording booth.

Placing her bag on the floor, she picked up the headphones from the desk and wandered over to the microphone. Her heart raced as she awaited her instruction and cue from the sound engineer. Taking his instructions through the headset, Emily began her script.

After almost an hour, and satisfied with her performance, Emily headed out of the booth. She wandered back through the waiting room's ambience and towards the exit. Smiling to herself, she pushed the revolving door onto the street. The warm summer rain wet her cheeks, and droplets rolled down her nose as she walked along the tree-lined street. Emily pulled her jacket around her neck and headed towards the safe haven of the multi storey car park.

How she had wished that she could have called Jake to tell him everything at that moment, but she had managed three weeks without him, returned every gift that had arrived at the house and had blocked his number from her phone. To open up any level of communication with him would thrust her back into the messed up relationship that she was trying to avoid.

It still didn't stop her missing his support. Taking her mobile from her phone, Emily scrolled through her contacts and stared at Jakes number on the screen. Her thumb poised over the red call symbol almost as if it had a mind of its own. Taking a few seconds to consider the call, her mind took back control of her heart and she found another number to call in its place.

"Hey Mum! Just got out of the studio and I am pleased with how it went! I know. It's been a few weeks but I have been busy at work and now with rehearsing for this second job, I just fall into bed." Emily explained, defending her reasons for not being in contact for a while. "Has he? Well that's kind of him but Jake and I aren't together any longer Mum. He isn't what you think he is. If you knew how he really was you wouldn't say that. I know he looked out for me, but I can do that for myself! I don't want to argue about it but I really am better off without him. I only called to share my news about the job and not for relationship counselling!' Emily exclaimed. "Got to go now, love you too. Bye!"

Eventually reaching the car, Emily pressed the unlock button on the key fob, pulled open the door and sank into the isolation of the driver seat. It was almost as if Jake had become the subject and centre of attention of almost everything that had happened over the past few years. He stole every moment of happiness that she had achieved and hijacked it for his selfish needs. Why was he even visiting her parents now that they were over? He had no rights to check up on her that way and to brainwash them into becoming his psychological messengers. They had no clue about the real Jake, just the fake Jake that presented himself at their door. In the heat of the moment, Emily unblocked his number and sent him a text.

"We are over, Jake, so leave my parents alone. Stop preying on their good nature. Don't even try to contact me as you are blocked on my phone, and stop trying to buy me with gifts. I don't want them, and I don't want anything more to do with you!"

Blocking his number again, she pushed the phone into her bag, turned on the ignition and headed out of the car park towards home. Having eventually reached the comfort of her flat after almost two hours of driving and being stuck in evening traffic, Emily poured a much-needed glass of cold white wine from the fridge and relaxed onto the settee. She was halfway through a film and a Chinese takeaway when a gentle knock at the door had disturbed her evening. Pulling herself up from the comfort of the settee, she wandered the hallway to find a teary eyed Jake stood at the door and looking somewhat bedraggled.

"Please don't close the door on me, Em. I just want to talk. I know we are over, but I just need to know that we can stay friends. That is all I came here for. Not to try to convince you otherwise. I haven't slept properly for weeks after what I did. I have talked to the doctor for help with my outbursts, and I want you to know that I am truly sorry for what I did." He blurted out as Emily had tried to shut the door. "Can I come in? I won't take too much of your time. I promise?" he continued to plead.

Against her better judgment, she invited him in on the understanding that it was just for a short while. Jake burst into tears and thanked her for her kindness. He spent the remainder of the hour talking about his past. He told her so much that she didn't know and felt a certain level of empathy for his broken soul. Emily spoke openly about why she thought things had gone so wrong. About how sorry she was that it was over and how she had hoped that Jake would get all the help he needed to get over his past. Happy that Jake understood that they had no future relationship together, Emily said her goodbyes refusing his request for a last hug and kiss.

Emily spent the next few weeks working herself stupid between the call centre and the studio after a new gig had been agreed through the agency. This time it was an audiobook role that would absorb weeks, possibly months, of her life, and the pay was almost double what she had expected. She was so exhausted from the long hours of rehearsing her lines and roles until the early hours of the morning, travelling to the studio and then fitting her call centre shifts around her work, that she had no time to spend with her friends. She spent almost all her time alone.

Emily had also received a more than generous payment from her advert role and another large monthly wage from her current voice-over role. With another offer for work already coming in from Voloquent, She handed in her notice at the call centre and promised to schedule in at least one or two weekends a month for a girl's night out with a sobbing Tammy. Relaxing into the extra time that she had to herself, she found time to re-join the gym, catch up with old friends and spoil herself with a day at the spa. She also put a deposit down on a five-star all-inclusive holiday for her and Tammy. Life was so good, and everything seemed so perfect.

Everything was going along smoothly until Emily's card was declined during an expensive shopping spree in London. Checking her online banking app, she noted that her expected monthly wage from Voloquent had not been paid on time. Contacting the bank to see if there was an error with their system, she was referred to her employer to verify the situation with her wages.

Locating their head office number, Emily was connected to a bubbly receptionist who was eager to help. Transferring her to the HR department, she waited patiently while listening to the most horrendous hold music. After what felt like an eternity, she was eventually connected.

"Can I take your employee number, please?" requested the assistant. "You will find it labelled "Our Reference" at the top right-hand corner of any communication we have sent you."

Looking through her email, Emily recited the number back to the women.

"Sorry that number doesn't appear to be on the system. Can you recite it again for me, please?"

Obligingly, Emily recited the number again slowly in case there had been any errors and waited patiently for her to locate her employee details.

"I am sorry, but there seems to be a problem. That number is definitely not on our system. Could you confirm how long you have been working for us?" she insisted.

"Of course! I have been working for you for a few months now. I had an email from you confirming my employment and have been in the studio recording my voice-overs as requested by your client. I have emails to prove that this is the case. I have also received wages from you directly into my bank account. There must be a mistake. Can you check again, please, or could I speak with your manager?" Emily said, confused by what she was being told.

"I am sorry, Miss White, but I don't appear to be able to find your details. I will just get my manager." And with that, Emily was put on hold again.

Her heart raced as the hold music continued its horrendous assault on her ears. Relax, she thought to herself. It's all a mistake. She knew how call centres worked. Sometimes, she had to try various ways to find a client's account while in her

56

previous role. After a few minutes had passed, a gentleman's voice appeared at the end of the line.

"Miss White, my name is Adrian. I am the HR Manager and deal with the staff cast's monthly wages through Voloquent. Could I take a few details from you so that we can help get this misunderstanding sorted?" he said calmly.

Feeling a little relieved that he was sure that he could help, Emily answered all his questions and gave her contact number so that he could return her call. She rifled through her purse to see if she could find enough change and wandered to a coffee shop to buy a warm, comforting drink while she waited. Placing her order at the counter, Emily took a seat at the window and watched as crowds of shoppers hurried past. It felt like an eternity as she stared at her phone and waited for his return call. A young waitress gave her a smile, placed a frothy coffee and a complimentary biscuit in front of her then headed back behind the counter.

Finally, after around twenty minutes, her mobile sprung to life.

"Hello, Is that Miss White? It's Adrian here from Voloquent. Are you able to talk?" he said in his calm manner.

"Hi Adrian, Yes, it's fine. Did you get to the bottom of things? Only I have my rent due this week, and I am currently in London overnight, so need to be able to buy my evening meal and pay my hotel bill," she said with worry.

"I am sorry, Miss White, but there appears to be a problem. I have searched our records, and even though we do have you on our system, we have not had any offer of work for you," came his reply.

Emily sat in silence. She couldn't quite get her head around what he was saying. She had been in the studio. She had been paid from Voloquent. How could it possibly be a fraud?

"I don't understand what you are telling me. I have received an email from yourselves confirming the job offer, then a script and been recording at the studio plus received payments from you for the work that I have already completed. How can that be possible if you are telling me that I was never offered the job in the first place, and you have never paid me?" Emily replied, fighting back the tears in confusion.

"I can imagine that this is really difficult to understand, and I am trying to get my head around it too, but we have definitely not had any requests for your voice. I have looked through our payroll system, and we have not sent any payments to your account details. It appears that you have been the victim of a cruel hoax," Adrian continued. "Can you confirm if you have spoken with anyone from our office over the past few months?"

"I haven't spoken to anyone. I received contact from a representative of Voloquent through my Linked In profile and responded directly to their message, providing my email address. All correspondence has been via Email. This is usually how things happen as per my past job with your company. Give me a second, and I can tell you the name of the person on I received the initial message from," she advised, as she searched through her online profile. "Ms. R Emerey, Recruitment officer," that's who contacted me. I even checked her LinkedIn profile, and it stated that she has worked for your company for several years," confirmed Emily.

"I am sorry, but I have worked in this department for almost twenty years, and we have never had anyone by that name working here at Voloquent," Adrian advised.

Emily was now in tears of frustration at the whole situation. So who exactly had she been working for, and what was all that recording stuff all about. Where did that actually go?

58

"Miss White, I would like you to forward all the information that you have to the police so they can follow this up as we do not want this happening to anyone else. This is a serious case of fraud, and it needs to be resolved," Adrian stated and waited for Emily to agree. After a few minutes of waiting for her to reply, he repeated his words.

Emily didn't hear a word that Adrian had said. She couldn't understand what was happening. Tears smudged her fresh makeup, and her mind tried to make sense of what she was being told. She was utterly lost in confusion. Why would anyone do such a thing to her? Why would they pay her for doing something that was not real?

"Miss White? Miss White? Are you still there? Could I pass your details onto the police for them to contact you?" Adrian persisted.

Emily agreed, said her goodbyes and placed her phone on the table next to her coffee cup. She sat in complete silence and tried to consider what had happened. She flicked onto her online banking app and scrolled to the payments she had received just to check that they were actually real. There, in black and white, were the payments coming into her account from Voloquent.

Then, reality of the enormity of the situation hit home and her heart sank. How the hell was she going to pay her hotel bill and, more to the point, how was she going to cover her monthly rent? She had nothing in her account and now had no job having given up her position in the call centre. What the hell was she going to do?

Chapter 8

Moving On

The police had visited Emily at the flat and taken a statement from her to assist with the investigation. They advised that it could take a few weeks before giving her any answers as it wasn't a typical fraud case. They suggested that she take things easy for a few days until the shock of the situation had settled. They gave her the telephone number for victim support just in case she needed to talk things over and get some help for what had happened. Emily thanked the police officers, followed them down the hallway and closed the door behind them.

Taking a mug from the cupboard, she poured herself an orange juice and pulled out her mobile from her pocket. Sinking into the comfort of her settee, she tried to think of what she needed to do. She had direct debits that needed to be cancelled until she found another job, and she needed to work out a budget so that she didn't overspend. She also needed to tell Tammy that their planned holiday was off, as she could no longer afford to go and needed to try to claim a refund to pay her rent. She also needed to speak with somebody to try to make sense of what had happened. Dialling Tammy's number, she felt so relieved to hear her cheerful voice at the end of the phone.

After downloading what had happened through her sobs and tears, Tammy had told her to get the kettle on. She must have run the route as in no time she was knocking at Emily's front door. Letting in a puffing and panting Tammy, Emily handed her a mug of tea and took a seat on the settee.

"This is just so messed up! I can't even begin to understand what the hell is going on!" Emily blurted out. "I just don't get why anyone would pay me for doing something that is not genuine and for no financial gain, unless they are selling my voice on the black market!"

"Try not to get worked up about it, Em. You got paid, didn't you? Does it matter who paid you? The police have all the details and will keep you informed the moment that they find anything out. I know this is absolutely crazy, but you will get through it, and I will be here to support you all the way! I am guessing that we will need to cancel that holiday, but that is cool. We can go when things settle down. Greece isn't going anywhere, and you need that money elsewhere right now!" reassured Tammy.

"Thanks, Tammy. I really appreciate you being so understanding and supportive. I have gone over and over the email that I have received, and everything seemed to be so normal. I had no reason not to believe that the job offer was fake. Why would I? Everything seemed legit and above board. They even confirmed all the details at the studio. It is driving me insane trying to figure this one out," Emily stated in disbelief.

So have you started to look for anything else just yet? You will need another job to keep this place going, I am guessing, unless you have a stash of cash hidden under your mattress?" questioned Tammy.

"I am already late with the rent, and in all reality, it looks as if I am going to have to give this place up. It is a charming home, but the rent is so high, and I can't be dealing with the added stress right now. I am sure that I can find somewhere more affordable and just as nice," said Emily, feeling deflated by the whole situation.

"If only my landlord would take cats, and I could evict my lazy housemate!" Tammy said, scratching a purring Jasper under the chin as he made himself comfortable on her lap. "Have you spoken to Jake? He has loads of space at his house, doesn't he? Maybe he could offer you an entire wing as a refuge in your time of need after everything that he put you through? Your still friends, aren't you?" Tammy continued.

"I don't know, Tam. I just don't want him to get the wrong idea. He is pretty messed up, and I would rather not get into anything I can't get out of. I guess I have to figure this one out for myself. The hardest thing is finding somewhere that will take Jasper!" Emily replied as she reached over to stroke his head.

"Even if he could just take Jasper for you! That would give you a bit more freedom. Just imagine he would be living in a palace surrounded by the countryside. What more could a beautiful little pussy cat want, hey? Hey?" Tammy said as she spoke directly to Jasper, who, at that moment, was enjoying the extra attention he was getting.

After about an hour, Tammy had said her goodbyes, and Emily got straight online. She searched through the property websites, looking for anything that she could possibly afford and could see herself living in. Nothing compared to her current flat and nowhere she did like, accepted pets. Picking up the phone, she reluctantly dialled Jakes number and waited for him to pick up.

"Hi, Emily. It's so good to hear from you!" came his reply.

"Hi, Jake. I have a huge favour to ask! I wouldn't ask if I had any other option, but it looks like I might have to move, and it's almost impossible to find anywhere which allows pets. You can say no, and I won't be offended, but would you be able to offer Jasper a temporary home. It's just until I get sorted?" Emily inquired.

"Of course! We can always do with his hunting skills around the manor, and you know how much I adore him. He will be well looked after here and eat like a king. But why are you moving? I thought you loved it there?" questioned Jake.

"Thank you! Thank you so much!" she exclaimed. "It's a long story and something that I don't really want to go into just now. But it will only be for a short time. Can I bring him around this evening?"

"I am out of the country at the moment, but I am sure if you leave him with Isobel, she will spoil him rotten. It is so good to hear your voice Em. Can we catch up soon?" he suggested.

"Thank you, Jake! I will pop him around there this evening, as I can't bear long goodbyes. I am so glad that we can remain friends after everything. Enjoy your trip, and maybe we can have a drink when you get back for old time's sake." And with that, Emily hung up.

Emily hunted for Jasper's cat carrier and filled it with his blanket and cat toys. Pushing him inside and zipping up the entrance flap, she placed his food from the cupboard, his ceramic paw print bowls and igloo cat bed into a carrier bag, then, headed for the car. The journey to Jake's home seemed to take no time at all. Stepping out of the car, she opened the rear door and pulled out Jasper's cat carrier along with his belongings and headed for the door.

Ringing the intercom, Isobel's cockney tones welcomed her and, within a few moments, she had appeared at the door.

"Hi, Isobel. Jake has told me to leave Jasper with you, as he will be staying here while I get myself sorted. His food, bowls and bed are all in the bag. If there are any problems, please call me, and I will come to collect him. Here's my business card with my number on it," she said, passing the bag and the card to Isobel, who was already crouched down and chattering to Jasper through the carry case.

"I love cats! He will be well looked after by me, Miss Emily, don't you worry! We have plenty of mice around the manor for him to chase. He won't come to any harm here, I tell you, not if I have anything to do with it!" Isobel answered as she stood to receive his belongings.

"That's so good to hear, Isobel. He is like my best friend, and it will be so strange not to have him around for a while. It's nice to know he will be spoilt." Emily said as she bent down to say her goodbyes. A lump appeared in her throat, and her eyes began to well up making her stand up abruptly and want to leave. "Could you ask Jake to call me when he gets back from his trip?" Emily smiled at a confused Isobel.

"Is he going somewhere?" Isobel questioned.

"Isn't he always!" Emily replied, remembering that Isobel's memory was not as sharp as it used to be, according to Jake.

"Thank's again, Isobel. Be sure to call me if Jasper gets into any trouble." With that, Emily turned and headed for the car.

Taking a seat inside the car, the tears ran uncontrollably down her face as she felt the pain of leaving her feline friend at his temporary foster home. Jasper had always been there for her to chat with. He gave her company when she didn't really want to see anyone. He had been there to hug after a bad day and soaked his fur with many of her tears over Jake. And she now felt as though she was abandoning him.

Taking a few moments to allow the tears to dry up, she turned on the engine, put on some music to distract her mind, spun around on the drive and headed towards the flat.

Emily spent the next few days viewing properties and applying for jobs. Nothing seemed successful. The jobs were either already taken, or she was over qualified. Every property she visited was too big, too small, riddled with damp or just on the "wrong" side of town. The only property that she had found was a potential flatshare with someone who worked nights. The flat was not the most welcoming, but it was close to the centre of town, the rent was low and, with the other tenant working nights, she would have the place to herself most of the time.

With all this considered, Emily decided that the flatshare was her best option and accepted the tenancy. She reluctantly handed in her notice at her flat and started the daunting task of downscaling her belongings to fit into the new place. It was incredible how much stuff she had accumulated over the years. Taking a few boxes of bric a brac to the local animal rescue charity. Selling off a pile of her designer clothes online to cover the cost of a self-hire removal van, Emily had managed to pack her entire life into one measly journey.

Jake had been in contact to give an update on Jasper and had insisted on helping her to move. After several trips up and down the eleven flights of stairs due to the lift being out of order, Emily slumped into the familiar comfort of the sofa-bed that almost filled the dreary room as Jake placed a box containing her cooking utensils onto the work surface of the shared kitchen.

"Are you sure your going to be alright here Em? It's not very...ummm...homely, is it?" Jake said as he appeared at the doorway. "You have never actually told me why you needed to move in the first place?"

"It will do for now. I can get some fresh flowers and brighten the place up a bit, and it will be fine. Hopefully, it's not forever. I am not going into it right now, Jake. I am too tired," she replied, trying to be positive as she looked around the empty walls.

"I have told you that you can stay with me. No strings attached purely platonic, unless just maybe you have changed your mind?" he probed.

"Jake, you know what I have said. I am happier about being friends right now. I just want to get myself sorted, and then who knows!" Emily replied assertively, hoping that Jake understood that there was still nothing between them.

"Fine, fine! I just don't like to see you like this. You deserve so much better, and I know that I can offer you that! But be as stubborn and pig-headed as you like. At least Jasper is living it up in luxury!" he smiled in response.

"How is my little man? I miss him so much. As soon as I get myself on my feet again, he will be out of your way and back on my lap where he belongs!' announced Emily.

"That's if he wants to! Isobel is fattening him up on her leftovers, and he slinks about as if he owns the place. He has even softened my father's heart, and that is something I have never seen before. But then I guess cats can charm the hardest of people into surrender with their false ways," Jake announced. "Right, I best be off. I have a date tonight!" he winked. "Call me if you need anything!" and with that, he disappeared.

Emily felt a pang of jealousy fill her chest. Did she hear him right? He had a date. How could he after just a few weeks? He had persistently told her he was devastated that they were no longer together and was waiting for her to change her mind. At that moment in the surrounding of this unfamiliar flat, Emily felt alone.

Chapter 9

Caught Out!

Emily had thrust herself into making her new place feel a little more welcoming. Her room was not huge, but it was functional. She added a few familiar pictures to the walls, placed rose petal scented candles on the windowsill, changed the curtains and fitted her crystal droplet lampshade to create a bit of elegance to the room. It had all given the room a different feel, although it still lacked that homely feel of her old place.

The bathroom stank of stale urine. The room was grubby, stained and very neglected. Discarded empty shampoo bottles and cardboard toilet roll tubes littered the floor. Emily had no intention of taking a bath in the filthy grim that stained the bathtub and the limescale deposits that clouded the silver taps. Putting on her marigold gloves and armed with almost every cleaning product that she could afford, Emily went to war. Spending a few hours with her face screwed up and trying to stop herself from vomiting as she removed pubic hair from the bathplug, Emily scrubbed the mouldy tiling grout with an old toothbrush until it sparkled white again. Then, bleaching almost every surface that she could find, the room had started to feel a little more hygienic and acceptable.

Taking a few moments break before tackling the kitchen, Emily flicked on the kettle and waited for it to boil. Exhausted from the physical assault the cleaning had taken out on her body, she flopped on the hardness of the wooden kitchen chair and looked at the bleakness of her surroundings. The kitchen was tiny and barely big enough for one person. It had just a small window next to the kitchen table that let in a little daylight. It was covered in a dirty grey net curtain and looked into the window of the flat next door. Looking downwards she could see into the smallest courtyard below that was filled with discarded cans, bottles and a pink plastic dolls pram. She missed the balcony at the old flat with its green open views. Here she felt claustrophobic and completely hidden from existence. Her mobile rang, breaking her sad thoughts. An unknown number flashed up as she hurried to answer it.

"Hello, Emily speaking!" she announced.

"Hello Miss White, this is DC Stapleton. I am calling concerning the recent fraud activity that we are currently investigating on behalf of Voloquent. We are following up some information about the case and would like you to come down to the station if it's not too inconvenient," came a soft female voice at the end of the line.

"Of course. When would you like me to come down? I am free most days," offered Emily.

"Are you able to come this afternoon, or is that too much short notice?" came the response.

"This afternoon is fine. Thanks. Bye," she responded as the officer hung up.

Emily's heart raced as she wondered exactly what they had managed to find out and what they needed from her. Quickly, she took a shower to cleanse the sweat and bathroom grim from her body and, throwing on an oversized jumper, a pair of jeggings and comfy boots, she headed to the police station.

The walk had lifted her spirit a little as the September breeze was still warm, yet, she could smell the dampness and decay of the coming season. A few golden leaves had already started to drift down from the trees above, announcing the arrival of autumn. Emily loved the colours that burst from the canopies at this time of year. It was almost nature's way of giving one last burst of beauty before letting go and giving in to winter. A few squirrels ran across her path frantically collecting their nutty harvest and burrowing them deep into the flowerbeds ready for their hibernation.

Eventually reaching the police station, Emily pushed open the door and walked towards the friendly police officer that stood behind the protective glass at reception.

"Hi, Can I help you?" she said as she smiled at Emily.

"I have received a call from a DC Stapleton requesting my assistance. My name is Emily White," she announced.

"Please take a seat, and I will advise DC Stapleton that you have arrived," the woman motioned towards the well-worn chairs in the corner of the office.

Nodding politely, Emily took a seat as requested. After just a short period, the adjoining door swung open, and a woman dressed in smart office attire presented herself as DC Stapleton.

"Come this way, Miss White, and we will find a room for us to talk further," she smiled and held the door open for Emily to follow.

This was the first time Emily had ever been inside a police station apart from to the front counter to hand in a purse she had once found on a bench in the local park. She had always wondered what had gone on in the back area that was hidden from public view. Following the woman officer, Emily wandered past a few policemen who nodded in acknowledgment as they sat at their desks, busy taking calls or tapping frantically into their computers. A printer burst to life, spewing out countless pages of text as a woman officer stood by, patiently waiting for it to complete its printing cycle.

DC Stapleton opened the door to the interview room and asked Emily to take a seat as another officer joined them.

The room was no bigger than a cupboard. She took a seat on one of the three comfortable blue office chairs surrounding a central table. DC Stapleton and her colleague took a seat opposite.

"Miss White, Emily White. Can I call you Emily?" said DC Stapleton.

"Of course. That's fine," Emily replied, as the other officer tapped away on a computer that sat on the table.

"We have asked for your presence as part of our investigations into the fraud allegations made by Voloquent concerning your current situation. They have identified you as the victim, so please be aware that this is just a formality and an opportunity to chase up a lead that we have on the case. My colleague, DC Rees, will be joining us today and taking a few notes so that we have all the details that we need to press charges," DC Stapleton announced as she tapped away on the computer.

Emily nodded to confirm that she understood and waited for them to continue.

"I have been made aware of the details that led you to contact Voloquent, which brought the circumstance to light. I need to confirm a few details about your recent acquaintances, and if it had been possible anyone had access to your personal details," DC Stapleton continued. "Can you please confirm the names of anyone that you feel are close enough to be able to obtain this information, access your laptop, bank details, etc.?"

Emily thought back over the past few months and considered who could have had any access to her details. Tammy had known her bank account details as she had given them to her to pay back some monies that she had borrowed. She would not have done that surely as she had been so excited about going on holidays, plus Tammy had no clue about her online profile with Voloquent ahead of the job offer. She had bought many things online, but that was just her debit card details and address, not her emails or social media accounts. The only person who could have accessed her laptop or phone had been Jake. He was always on there checking her messages.

Relaying those thoughts to the officers, DC Stapleton continued her questions.

"Could you please advise us of his full name and when your relationship began?" she inquired.

"His full name is Francis Jacob Eddersley, but he legally changed his first name to Jake," Emily replied as both officers looked at each other.

"We are aware of Mr Eddersley and have had dealings with him in the past, albeit of a different circumstance," DC Stapleton announced. "Please continue!"

Emily continued with her account of their relationship as DC Rees frantically took everything down on the A4 note pad that lay in front of him. After almost an hour of questions, reliving accounts of her up and down relationship with Jake and his controlling character, DC Stapleton finally stood up and thanked Emily for her time and confirmed that her information had been beneficial to their investigations. Walking her back through the office, DC Stapleton advised her not to speak with Mr Eddersley if at all possible for the immediate future and, opening the security door into reception, they both said their goodbyes.

Emily headed out into the fresh air. Her mind was spinning. Did they think that Jake was capable of fraud? She hadn't even considered that he could have been the one to fake the whole situation, but she also wouldn't have put it past him.

But it was all too crazy even to consider. How had he managed to send her an email from the Voloquent office? The police had found no evidence that the emails had come from another location, either. Emily had been in a daydream for almost back to the flat as she tried to work everything out. Noting the lift was out of order again, she wandered up the eleven flights of stairs, pushed the key in the door and shut out the world behind her. Kicking off her shoes and placing her coat on the hook, Emily headed back into the kitchen to make the coffee that still sat in the cup unused from a few hours previously.

Flicking on the kettle to re-boil the water, Emily sank into the uncomfortable hard wooden kitchen chair and warmed her hands on the mug, taking away the seasonal chill. An empty tin of beans sat on the countertop, reminding her that she was not alone in the house. She had still not met the other tenant, but he had a habit of leaving these lazy reminders that he was very much present. She found Colin's lack of presence creepy. He was possibly spying on everything she did without her even knowing. Her body shook uncontrollably at the thought. She needed to get out of this place as fast as she could. It's bleakness starting to seep into her soul. At that moment, the ringing of her mobile made Emily jump.

"Miss White. This is DC Stapleton. I wish to inform you that we have arrested Mr Eddersley this afternoon in connection with the fraud allegations that we have received from Voloquent," came the voice at the end of the phone.

Emily didn't hear anything else. She was trying to take in the enormity of what she had just heard.

"Miss White, are you still there. Did you hear what I said? He will be charged and then released until the court hearing. This man is known to us to be a threat to women. I would advise you not to have any dealings with Mr Eddersley for your safety,' the voice continued. "If, for any reason, you feel in danger, please do not hesitate to contact us." The line went dead.

It almost felt as if the world had opened up and swallowed her at that moment. Emily felt nothing but fear and panic race through her entire body. What did they mean he was a threat? He had raised his voice a few times and kicked the door, but he had never actually physically harmed her.

Had Jake really been guilty of false representation, faking a job and paying her a wage for work that didn't exist? He had wanted to command all her time and attention, and this was one way of getting it. Yet they had not even been together for the past few weeks, so how was this worth his while? So had the sudden change in his character been all part of the plan? It would have made sense.

He had become more distant, been more understanding and happy to help her with everything. Telling her she needed her own space and independence, but the whole time deceiving her, hoping to gain complete control of her life. He had managed to get Emily to hand in her resignation from a job he had not wanted her to have, but that she had loved for a job that never existed. This had then destroyed her regular social life that Jake had always been so jealous of. Had he really paid her an obscene wage from his bank account to be in control of almost every aspect of her life? If this was all true, he had even tried to convince her to move in with him. Was he planning on making her his prisoner?

Then, to top it all off, she had been warned that he was a potential threat and advised to stay away from him. Emily shuddered at the whole situation. It was messed up. She needed to get out. She needed a strong drink. Grabbing her jacket, Emily made her way to Tammy's.

Chapter 10

Runaway

It had almost been a week since Jake's arrest. Emily had received numerous grovelling texts from Jake with lame apologies, but she ignored every message he sent. Her mother was so ashamed for not believing her daughter's judgement of character.

"He was so convincing, Em. It was hard not to believe everything he said. We thought he was your perfect match, and you would have been a fool to let him go. Just shows that I am not great at judging people, which frightens me," Emily's mother had stated when she had broken the news to her.

Emily herself still couldn't get to grips with what had happened. It was all so messed up that it felt like some weird twist of fate thriller that she would have watched on Netflix with a bowl of popcorn and gasped at the revelation. But this was not a movie. This was real and had happened to her. Her mind just had no way of accepting that Jake was that manipulative. She knew that he was controlling and demanding but to manipulate her mind in that way was just sick. What she still hadn't worked out was why he was a known potential threat to women.

Tammy had promised to do some digging and try to find out anything from her access to archived records at University and was full of "I told you so's" when she found out was Jake had been up to.

"He was creepy, Em. Stalking you and controlling everything you did. Just think back through everything. He was pretty manipulative from day one. Love bombing you with so many compliments, expensive holidays and gifts. He had your mind programmed into complete blindness. But man, he is a pretty interesting character from my perspective. Maybe I can do my thesis on this for my final degree. The mind of a predator!!" Tammy announced as she considered the thought. "You need to get away for a while. Give your mind a break from everything. Now is the time for that Greek holiday if ever there was a need for one."

Tammy was right, Emily thought. She would do anything to get away at that very moment. Life had taken a complete nose dive since she had met Jake. There had been some highs, but almost every high was preceded by a low. She had just wished that she had not fallen for his cheeky charisma that night at the club.

That's how she had gotten to this very point in her life, jobless, single, penniless, flat sharing with Creepy Colin, who she had still not met, in a place she hated and without her feline friend Jasper. Life was at rock bottom, and Emily hated every aspect of it.

A text from Tammy vibrated against her thigh as she wallowed in the self-pity of the moment.

"Girl, I have done some digging, and you wouldn't believe what I have found out! Call me. It is going to fry your brain!"

Picking up the phone, she immediately dialled Tammy's number and waited for her to answer.

"Em! My God. We should have checked this guy out the minute I had my suspicions, and you wouldn't have gone through this mess. I am going to send you a link to a newspaper article that I have found. It's all a bit crazy, but you had a lucky escape! Call me back when you have read it. Got to Go. The tutor has arrived." And with that, Tammy vanished.

A text with just a solitary kiss and two separate internet links attached, beeped through her mobile. Emily pressed on one link and was instantly transported to a small newspaper article from a few years previous in the local paper. She began to read,

"Shortly after 11pm, Police officers were called to Beech Avenue following a report that a vicious assault had been carried out on a woman in her early twenties by the accused, Mr Francis Eddersley on the night of the 12th May. The victim, Miss Katy James, suffered several stab wounds to her arms and chest and further head injuries from the assault. The accused was also arrested on suspicion of several other offences related to separate incidents – these include ABH to the victim's partner, Mr Nick Davies, failing to stop for police, dangerous driving, and criminal damage to a police vehicle. Inspector Tom Haver said: "This was a nasty incident caused through jealous rage after the victim had made countless reports of harassment and stalking. This has left the victim requiring hospital treatment for her injuries. Fortunately, these are not believed to be life-threatening. This type of violence is not acceptable. The accused has been remanded in custody until a hearing of the case has been appointed."

Emily suddenly felt sick. She couldn't believe what she was reading. Surely this was a mistake as Jake had told her that his ex-girlfriend was the stalker. Katy was the crazy one who had an affair. Jake had convinced Emily that he had been the victim and that he had done nothing wrong. Emily pressed on the next link.

"Francis Jacob Eddersley appeared at Guildford crown court charged with GBH, dangerous driving, failing to stop and criminal damage. The case relates to an incident at the home of Miss Katy James on the evening of 12th May, which left the victim suffering multiple stab wounds to the chest and arms, plus head injuries from the unprovoked attack. Mr Eddersely had visited the home of the victim after hearing that she had started a new relationship. The victim had disclosed that she had endured regular emotional and physical abuse during the two years they had been together, resulting in her receiving counselling and therapy. This had been the reason why she had chosen to end their relationship.

The defendant pleaded not guilty on the grounds of a psychiatric assessment. During sentencing, the courts determined that his unstable mental health had impaired his judgement. The offender was given a suspended two-year sentence to allow him to undergo a probation and rehabilitation period. If the defendant breaches the terms of his sentence or commits another offence, then he will serve the original prison term imposed."

Emily's mind could not take in the words that she had been reading. The incident had taken place just a few months before they met. Why had she not walked away as soon as she felt things were not right? Emily wandered into the kitchen and flicked on the kettle. Her mind went over everything that she had been through in the past few years. The lies he had told, the need for control, the deceit and the emotional bullying, not forgetting the anger she had witnessed, they were all red flags to the monster that she had allowed into her head and heart. Emily had also seen a side to Jake that appeared soft and injured, just like a wounded animal that she had wanted so much to heal and fix. He was even more messed up than she had even considered, she thought as she poured the coffee and headed back into her bedroom.

Emily wandered to the window and looked through the rain-smudged glass into the greyness beyond. A gust of wind howled between the trees in the garden sending a flurry of autumnal colours spinning onto the sodden grass.

"Sometimes I wish I could turn back the clock," she said to herself as she looked into the heaviness of the day, pulling the hot coffee mug into her chest.

The nutty aroma filled her lungs with a warming hug as she closed her eyes and drifted back to the distant haziness of the seemingly endless summers of her carefree youth. Magical evenings filled with laughter and dancing with lost friends as the scent of wild thyme and jasmine had intoxicated the warm evening air. Watching and hearing nothing but the chirping sound of the cicadas, as the setting sun had displayed a palate of vibrant colours over the watery horizon, capturing her soul. Endless lazy days on warm golden sands submersed in its heady coastal air entirely hypnotised by the sounds of perfectly formed turquoise waves crashing against the shore. The warmth of the Greek sunshine that had kissed her skin and sent shivers of bliss through her relaxed body. Those moments before her understanding of normality had been sucked from her very existence.

A sudden crashing noise jolted her back to the present moment and to the drizzly misery of late September in the UK. Taking a sip from her mug, Emily watched through the raindrops as two men struggled against the wind. Fighting against the elements to pick up a wheelie bin that had toppled over in its strong unforgiving gusts. She continued to watch as they emptied its decaying contents into the back of the refuse lorry. Days like these made reality a bit harder to cope with. Being cooped up with nothing to distract her mind made Emily mull over the events of the past few weeks. She still could not quite make sense of precisely what had happened. It was still almost too crazy to be real.

Emily turned her gaze from the window and wandered across to the well-loved sofa bed that filled the compact living space of her dreary room. She flopped herself into its perfectly formed seat pads, shaped over the years by her overly ample buttocks. Then, she curled her legs up and took another sip of coffee. Her mobile suddenly burst into life with the spine- chilling, melodic reminder of its sender. Taking out her phone, she read yet another grovelling text to add to the several messages she had already received that morning from Jake.

"Are you being serious? After everything we've been through together, you can't even be bothered to answer my calls or messages. One bad mess up and that's you done!"

This wasn't one terrible mess up. This had been the biggest mess-up of the century. Jake had utterly screwed with her mind and she wanted nothing more to do with him. Emily threw her mobile onto the empty seat beside her and glugged down the last of the coffee.

Flicking on the TV, she searched through the listings looking for anything to fill the morning void. Settling on "Homes under the Hammer," her mind was blissfully distracted for a few pointless minutes, as she watched the transformation of a dilapidated old council house to the perfect family home.

A knock at the door interrupted the crucial part where they gave a new value on the completed project. Standing up in a moment of frustration, Emily wandered the dimly lit hallway. She opened the door to a sweaty, red-faced and overweight deliveryman, awkwardly holding a bouquet of red roses and a bottle of Dom Perignon Champagne while trying to catch his breath.

"I...have a...delivery for...Miss Emily White." He paused, trying to regain control of his breath. "Could you...sign here... please?" he managed to blurt out between wheezes, then extending his digital signing pad into her empty hands. "Thanks!" he said as he thrust the delivery into her arms, swivelled on the spot, walked towards the first of eleven flights of stairs and reluctantly started his descent.

Emily momentarily remained in the doorway with her arms filled with the half-expected gift. She knew exactly who it was from without even needing to check the card. This is what he did. He always thought he could buy her forgiveness, but this time he had gone too far. After everything she had found out, there was no going back.

Taking the handwritten gift card out of the flowers, Emily placed the bouquet next to a full glass bottle of creamy milk on her elderly neighbours doorstep. Knocking their door, she wandered back into her flat. Putting the cold bottle of expensive champagne into an empty space in the wooden wine rack on top of the fridge freezer, she opened the small pink envelope and read the card.

"I am really sorry. Please forgive me. J X"

"Urgh!!" she grunted disapprovingly.

Pushing the pedal on the chrome waste bin, Emily threw the card inside and slammed it shut. Why couldn't he just leave her alone, she thought, as her mobile pinged again with yet another message from Jake.

"Do you like the flowers? I thought we could share the champagne tonight over dinner so I can explain? 7pm at mine?" his text read.

Emily had no intention of going anywhere near his house ever again. His money didn't impress her. His extravagant gifts, last minute holidays and meals out at expensive restaurants were just a distraction from the real Jake that she now knew. The Jake who had lost her, her job, her sanity and the reason why she was flat-sharing with creepy Colin, who only came out at night.

Chapter 11

Obsession

Emily sunk back onto the sofa and took a sip from her luke warm coffee. Yet another horrendous daytime show blurted out of the TV that sat on the dated chest of drawers positioned in the corner of her dismal bedsit. She couldn't cope with this for much longer. The monotony of endless days alone was starting to get to her. She needed a job. She needed to get out of the dreariness of this flat, this city and away from Jake's constant stalking, she thought as another pleading text popped up on the screen. Why couldn't he just get the message? She wasn't interested in his pleads, apologies or offerings. He needed severe psychological help, and she wasn't going to waste her life being treated as a possession. Her face reddened with anger at the thought of what he had done. Grabbing the phone, she typed another response.

"LEAVE ME ALONE!!!"

A sudden grip of panic tightened at her stomach as she blocked his telephone number on her mobile, stopping his ability to respond. Scanning through her social media apps on her phone, she removed him from her friend's list on all her accounts, deleting all the photographs and removing all evidence that he had ever existed. If only she could erase her memory that easily, she thought, as she watched the entire past year on her Facebook profile, disappear. Changing her status to single, Emily flopped backward onto the cushions feeling a moment of courageous accomplishment.

Rejecting Jake was not easy. It took all her determination to remain resilient to her own desires for the insane cycle she appeared to be stuck in. She had blocked Jake several times before, but his pursuit became more intense after each rejection. He had often shown up at the flat, drunk and in little control of his body, ending up in her bed with Emily underneath him. Then, life had just continued as if nothing had happened. But this time she wouldn't let him back in, she was adamant.

Emily took a deep breath. So what now? She thought to herself. A job, that's what she needed more than anything and some money coming in as her savings had almost but vanished. She checked her Linked in account for any recent job offers. Then typed "Local Jobs" into the search engine on her smart phone, in hope that something suitable would appear. She knew she would never find her dream career on these sites, so dismally scrolled endlessly through numerous unskilled jobs' that flooded her phone screen. Every one of them offering low paid, long shifts that would have completely taken over her every waking moment for little income. The state benefits she was now in receipt of, gave her more of an income than anything she had found remotely interesting. How had she ended up in this? Everything had been going so well for her.

If she hadn't taken that stupid job offer, then she would still be back in the call centre and dancing the weekends away with her work colleagues. Emily shoulders shuddered and her entire body shook at the thought of how naïve she had been. She hadn't realised how easily manipulated she could be. Shaking her head in disappointment, she pushed herself off the sofa and grabbed a towel from the hook on the back of the bedsit door.

Opening her door quietly, not to disturb creepy Colin, Emily snuck across the hallway to the safety of the bathroom. Quickly bolting the door behind her, she put the plug in the bath and turned on the hot tap. Taking the bubble bath from her side of the bathroom cabinet and drawing it towards her nose, she took in a deep breath of the salty aroma that burst from the bottle as she squeezed it, then poured the blue liquid into the hot running water. She watched as it changed the colour of the water into a deep aqua blue, reminiscent of the Mediterranean Sea during her most recent visit to the Greek islands. Steam filled the room as she removed her baggy t-shirt and saggy old joggers, then stepped cautiously into the warm inviting water.

Emily lent back as the water lapped up around her shoulders, giving her a comforting hug, as the bubbles tickled her chin before popping against her ears. The wind whistled through the poorly fitted glass accompanied by the drumming of the driving rain that viciously thrashed against the windowpane. Closing her eyes, she sighed then breathed in the heady ocean scent of the bubbles. Her lungs filled with the sensory experience and her mind drifted into an illusion of golden sands, turquoise seas and endless hot sunny days. Her body relaxed as she became consumed by the moment.

How she wished that her daydream had been her reality at that moment. Life always seemed easier in the sun. She could have dealt with everything better if she had been lazing on the beach whilst looking for answers. The perpetual greyness of the UK seemed to destroy any enthusiasm she had for living now that she lacked any reason to get out bed. It also gave her an excuse to hide herself away as she struggled with the after affects of her relationship with Jake. All her friends had been supportive, dropping by for coffee and offering their own accounts after their hectic days at work, but even they couldn't get their heads around what had happened to her. The more they talked about what had occurred, the more it sounded like a film of someone else's life. She had even visualised Anna Friel as the leading lady playing her part. Maybe even a book being written as it was all too crazy to actually be real.

Her mind wandered to the events of the past few months as she tried to find a reason to why she had not even contemplated that something had been wrong. She had always been taught by her mother that if something seemed to good to be true, then it mostly was. But she had lapped it up like a trusting puppy and never even considered she was being led on. How could anyone deceive her as much as he had, yet think that he had not done anything wrong, to the point that she really did not trust anyone at that moment. Emily had pretty much shut herself away into the safety of her dreary bedsit where she could hide away from life and Jake.

He must have been so desperate to keep her for himself. She had noticed his unhealthy obsession far too late. She had almost allowed Jake to take full control of her life, feeling sorry for him after his previous relationship. She had found him endearing at first, giving her all his time and affection. Nothing had been too much trouble for him. But very quickly into the relationship, everything had become suffocating and his constant demands for her attention was just too much to cope with. Yet her friends had never really listened to her concerns. When she brought up how she felt in conversation with them, they would be dismissive, telling her that she should be grateful, as they would do anything to have a boyfriend like Jake, who spent all his time and money on her.

He had even managed to turn her own mother against her, having her believe his accounts of Emily's infidelity, selfishness and betrayal. She would regularly wake up to a text from her mother, scorning her for something she had never actually done or said. To the point she had stopped answering her mothers calls and visiting her parents. They had approved of Jake as he had charmed them into believing he was a good catch. He treated their daughter like a princess, and in their defence, that's all anyone could ever want for their children. But his latest stint had shown his true colours to everyone as he failed to cover all his tracks. He had been tardy and managed to get caught out, exposing the truth.

Having spent a dreamy hour in the warmth of the bath water, Emily dried herself, dressed and made her way to the kitchen to make lunch. She opened the fridge door and looked dismally into its bleak coldness. Her shelf was almost empty apart from a few limp carrots, a small square of blue cheese wrapped in tin foil that had been there for months, an old shrivelled onion and a bunch of coriander that had started to go slimy on some of the leaves. Carrot soup it is then, she thought to herself, as she pulled the ingredients from the shelves and reached for the food processor. Busying herself with her food preparations, her mind focused on the task of creating lunch and stopped her thoughts from wandering to her dire financial state. Having followed the recipe from memory that had imbedded itself from her childhood Saturdays baking with her grandmother, Emily flicked on the kettle and lent against the kitchen counter.

She looked around the room and took in her surroundings. The kitchen units looked like they had been salvaged from a skip as the mustard yellow laminated cabinet doors all hung uneven on their frames. The surrounding black and white tiles would have been more suited to a public lavatory and the dirty grey lino tiles under her feet she was sure had not been replaced since the 1970s. An area of black damp filled the far corner of the ceiling above the units and a few patches had started to appear behind the hideous orange pine farmhouse table pushed into the far corner of the room. It was soulless and a far fetch from the modern chic of her old flat. But, it was better than nowhere even it was chilly and damp.

As the soup bubbled in the pan, she prepared the table for one. She took a seat and flicked through social media to see what her friends were up to. Everyone seemed to have plans for the weekend apart from her. She had little money to even consider a night out. Her hair hadn't been styled for weeks, her fake tan had faded and she needed her acrylics done to make her feel a little bit more like the Emily she had once known. The old Emily who had been the life and soul of the party before Jake had sucked the life out of her, and left her not trusting anyone.

Pushing herself up from the farmhouse chair, she took a bowl from the cupboard, ladled some of the thickened soup into the bowl, crumbled on the cheese and sprinkled the remains of the healthiest looking coriander leaves, on top. Cradling the bowl with both hands to warm her fingers, she took a seat and scooped the deep orange liquid into her mouth. The homely taste of the hot soup filled her body with warmth as the pungent cheese softly melted on her tongue. She closed her eyes and enjoyed the moment of comfort the soup gave her from the reality of her situation. How could she possibly change the rut she had found herself in? She also had to consider saving enough to move house again as Jake knew where to find her and that was worrying, after everything that she had found out.

Checking her phone again, Emily was pleased to see a message from an old university friend inviting her out for a coffee and a catch up. Taking advantage of the invite, Emily grabbed her coat and headed into the damp late autumn afternoon, relieved to be leaving the isolation behind.

Having spent a few hours in the company of her old university pal and accepting his offer to buy her a lager in the local pub, Emily said her goodbyes and headed out into the darkness. Zipping up her jacket and lifting the fur lined hood to shelter from the cold driving wind, Emily huddled into its welcome warmth. A fine drizzle soaked her face as droplets slowly rolled down her nose then dripped towards the ground. She pushed her hands into the deep pockets and made her way towards home. She hated nights like these.

The weather had never crossed her mind when she had been sat in a warm crowded pub or club, drinking copious amounts of alcohol to the point she couldn't even feel the cold or notice the rain. But tonight was different. Tonight she felt a million miles away from the person she had been just a few weeks previous. She had never left a pub that early sober neither had she ever left because she couldn't afford to buy herself a drink. Normally at that time on a Friday evening she would have already been drunk and crawling the pubs without ant concerns for money, the weather or the onset of winter. If anything she would have been looking forward to cosy winter nights and planning all those Christmas parties. Emily hated the position she had found herself in and the weather was not helping either.

Taking a short cut through the darkness of the park, Emily felt vulnerable. She had walked this park so many times by day but never alone by night. The vast numbers of bushes seemed to swallow her self-confidence. The park was empty and nothing stirred apart from the trees shedding the occasional leaf above. Her irrational mind stepped up a gear and everything became a potential threat. It was only a short walk but she felt as though she was being watched from the shadows of the tree trunks. The thought of Jake flooded her mind. She could feel her heart pounding in her throat as she passed by the memorial statue that now seemed so fearsome as it loomed over her. Her pace quickened as the safety of the streetlights ahead caught her vision.

Eventually reaching the park gates and emerging into the hustle and bustle of the Friday night work crowds, Emily let out a sigh of relief and continued her walk towards the flat. With just a few streets to go, Emily stopped by the local shop and found enough change in her purse for a pint of milk and a packet of space raider crisps. This was the highlight of her night. A milky coffee would warm her as she snuggled down alone to watch yet another repeat film on TV. How she wished Jasper had been there to greet her on arrival and to keep her company.

Reaching the front of the flats, Emily searched her bag for her keys, turned on the light on her mobile phone and headed down the side to the entrance of the flats. The ally way was dark and secluded. She started to panic again as she tried hastily to unlock the door. Suddenly, she felt an arm grab her from behind. Her mobile smashed to the ground and milk carton splashed its contents all over Emily's legs as the attacker pinned her arm to her side and covered her mouth stopping her from crying out. Emily felt the fear grip at her throat. She writhed about in their firm hold and tried to punch with her one free arm. She scratched at his face and kicked out with her legs as she felt herself being dragged backwards into the ally way. The breath of her attacker was warm over her face as the bristles of their unshaven face scratched at her cheek. Their hand pressed hard against her mouth and nose, so firmly that she could hardly breathe. The strength drained from her so quickly as she fought against them but the lack of oxygen made her feel faint.

"You think its OK to replace me that quickly? I saw you with him at the pub!" came a familiar voice. "It's obvious that you have been planning this all along with your slutty clothes. You are just like the rest of them. No respect for me, or anything I ever did for you. If I can't have you then no one will!"

Emily suddenly felt the wetness of the cold concrete floor against her cheek as her limp body hit the ground hard causing a cracking sound as her attacker kicked her in her side. She felt a sharp pain shoot through her chest whilst Jake continued to kick at her torso. She let out a howl in pain, then, felt the plastic tread of his trainer heavy on her face. She took the last of her strength to shout out before she completely passed out.

Chapter 12

Recovery

Emily woke in a state of confusion. Her head pounded and she winced with pain on each incoming breath. Her eyes were heavy and blurry as they tried to absorb her surroundings. Everything was bright making her squint. The initial muffled voices that seemed in the distance became closer and louder as she became more alert. The appearance of a womanly shape leaning over her caused her to panic and lash out.

"Emily, your safe. It's OK. Everything is fine. Please don't panic. I am a nurse" Came a calm female voice.

"Where am I?" slurred Emily through her swollen lips.

"You are in hospital. You were brought in last night. I am just doing the morning observations. Do you remember anything at all about last night?" the nurse asked as she checked took her arm to check her blood pressure.

"My mind is a bit fuzzy and my head hurts," she said squeezing her eyes shut to try and remove the blur from her vision that was making her feel queasy.

"You have suffered a head trauma and a few broken ribs, so you will be feeling a little uncomfortable," the nurse reassured.

"It was Jake! He attacked me. He grabbed me as I tried to unlock the door to the flat. I remember his voice and his hot breath against my cheek," Emily suddenly panicked.

"Your attacker was remanded in custody last night, so understand that you are safe. Your flatmate saved your life. He restrained your attacker, then, called the police and the ambulance.

"Colin? I have never even met my flatmate. Could I have a pain killer, my head is pounding," she said in disbelief.

"The police are waiting outside to speak with you. Do you think that you are up to it? If not I can ask them to come back later," the nurse questioned.

"It's fine. I will get it out of the way and then I can go back to sleep. I feel so tired," she announced.

"That's expected after a head injury. We did take you for a scan straight away last night and the consultant will be around this morning to read over the results. I will let them know you are ready to talk," and with that the nurse left the room.

Emily reached for the water on the table that was pushed over her bed. As she lifted her arm, a pain shot up her side and caused her to cry out. Cautiously moving the cup closer to her mouth, she felt the coldness of the liquid touch her broken skin as it trickled through swollen lips, refreshing her dry palette. She lowered her head back onto the comfort of the pillow that supported her back and neck and looked around the clinical brightness of the room. How she could have done with a warm mug of homely coffee. This had always given her a reason to pause and really absorb the moment. It seemed to make everything more comfortable no matter how bad the situation. Her mind couldn't quite take everything in without that perfect hug in a mug.

The noise of the door opening made Emily look directly at DC Stapleton, who entered with a colleague.

"Good Morning Miss White. I won't take up to much of your time as I fully appreciate that you will need to rest after your ordeal," she announced. "I can understand how hard this will be for you, so at anytime, if you wish to stop, just let me know. Now can you tell me everything that has happened since we last spoke," she said pulling up a chair next to Emily's hospital bed.

"There isn't much to say. I have had a few text messages from Jake apologising about what he did but I had not responded to any until yesterday morning when he sent a bouquet of flowers and expensive champagne to the house. He sent me a text almost immediately after the delivery inviting me to his house for a meal to apologise. I sent him a text telling him to leave me alone, removed him from my social media and blocked him from contacting me," Emily paused to take a sip of her water. "An old male university friend contacted me and invited me out for a coffee as I have been having a rough time financially since the revelation. I accepted and, after a few hours at the café, we ended up at the pub as it was Friday. I left after just one drink at around 8pm and made my way home. I took a swift short cut through the local park as I felt vulnerable in the dark."

"Did you notice anyone suspicious as you walked home?" DC Stapleton questioned.

"Not once did I consider I was being followed. It was raining, cold and dark. I was not bothered by my surroundings just hurrying to get out of the elements.," Emily announced.

"OK, Continue, that's if its not too painful," reassured the detective.

"Its OK. I remember reaching the front of the flats and fumbling in my bag to get my keys, then making my way down the lane that runs to the side of the flats. It's always dark there so I put on the spotlight of my phone. I tried to get the keys in the door but my hands were shaking with the cold. That's when he grabbed me. I didn't know who it was at first. He grabbed me from behind, smothered my mouth and nose so I could hardly breath let alone shout for help," Emily's voice started to panic.

Emily had returned to the reality of her memory as if she was actually reliving the terror of the moment.

"His unshaven face scratched at my cheek and I felt his breathe against my ear. Then he spoke in an aggressive manner. It was as if his teeth were gritted as I felt the shower of spit over my face before he let me drop to the floor and kicked my side over and over," she said as tears rolled down her face.

"Take a drink and pause for a moment Emily. You are doing great and I understand that this is all so recent which is why its important that we get the details as soon as possible from you," DC Stapleton said supportively. "Do you remember what he said to you?"

"I remember it so vividly," she responded immediately. "He said "You think its OK to replace me that quickly? I saw you with him at the pub! It's obvious that you have been planning this all along with your slutty clothes. You are just like the rest of them. No respect for me, or anything I ever did for you. If I can't have you then no one will!" Emily shuddered at the memory. "That's when I managed to shout out before I felt his foot on my face. That's when I blacked out. I don't remember anymore until I woke up in here," she said looking around the room.

"And the voice you heard. Can you identify who that was?" asked DC Stapleton.

"It was Jake. It was Jake Eddersley. I am 100% sure it was him even though I did not see his face. I remember scratching him and kicking him before I hit the ground but I couldn't get out of his grip. Why would he do this to me? Why?" tears ran uncontrollably down Emil's face as she felt the fear of the moment fill her body.

"You did nothing wrong Emily. This is not your fault. We will need to take some samples from under your fingernails as evidence. You were lucky your flatmate was on his way back from the gym when it happened. Without his intervention who knows how it could have ended. Is there anything else that you feel is relevant? If not we will leave you in peace so you can rest," she questioned.

"That's everything. I don't think that there is anything else. I was wondering if someone could contact my parents as my mobile was smashed during the attack," Emily requested.

"Of course. Let me know their address and we will send someone around," DC Stapleton smiled, as she stood up from the chair and said her goodbyes.

Emily nodded, closed her eyes and fell back into a deep sleep.

After a few days in hospital, Emily headed back to her parents to recover. She had received news from DC Stapleton that Jake had been charged and imprisoned with GBH and fraud. His sentence had been increased as he had breached the terms of his initial offence. This news had eased her anxiety and allowed her to relax a little and concentrate on her recovery.

In the first few days of being back at her parents Emily had received so many cards and gifts. Her closest friends, including Tammy, had visited and shown their support and shared their horror at what had happened to her. But the recovery was not easy. She would often wake with nightmares as she relived the memory of the attack over and over. The swelling and bruising had almost gone but the experience still gripped at her consciousness.

After a while, Emily had made the decision to hand in her notice at the flat and had returned, with Tammy as support, to collect her belongings. This had not been an easy exercise. Being back at the front door had given her a mild panic attack and she had needed a little while before pushing the key into the lock. As she pushed open the flat door, a smiling Colin had been stood in the kitchen making a cup of tea. This was the first time that she had actually seen her flatmate and now, her hero.

He was tall, dark and extremely handsome. His physique was taut from the dense muscle mass that he carried, as if he spent all his time working out at the gym. It was no wonder that he had detained Jake, long enough for the police to arrive. Without even a thought about creepy Colin that she had created in her mind, Emily rushed to give him a hug and thanked him for his help. After fighting off her attention and accepting the bottle of wine she had bought him, he brushed passed an ogling Tammy and disappeared back into his bedroom.

Emily packed up her belongings as she watched Tammy slip her number under Colin's door and wander back up the corridor smiling like a schoolchild.

"Well, you have to take a chance sometimes don't you! And him bein a hero and those muscles!" Tammy exclaimed as Emily shook her head at her brazenness.

Leaving the key on the kitchen counter, Emily pulled the door shut on her old life.

Chapter 13

New Adventures

It had been almost a month since her ordeal and Emily was still out of work. October had arrived with a vengeance and she spent empty days searching for answers to everything. She had heard that Jake had been placed in a prison in Newcastle and this gave her a certain level of reassurance that he wasn't going to appear at her door anytime soon.

But the nightmares and emotional scars still remained. Every time she applied for a job, she was met with an untrusting feeling that it was not real. This she couldn't shake. Jasper had also returned to live at her parent's house after her father had paid the Eddersley's a visit and after a few minutes negotiating with Isobel, she had reluctantly handed him over.

Being back with her parents was also a hard pill to swallow. Emily had been fiercely independent all her life and had not returned to live at her childhood home since leaving for university. She hated being dependant on them for money. She needed to build up her confidence again and to get back out there into the big wide world.

Her ordeal had also made her crave a new life in a new country. Call it running away, but Emily didn't care. She just knew that the further away so was, the more likely she could start over. This would also remove the memories that haunted her every time she took a walk to all the familiar places she had shared with Jake.

As Emily scrolled aimlessly through her social media one evening with a content Jasper curled up on her lap, an advert for a work away opportunity in Greece caught her eye.

"Eco farm-alternative energy-all female help wanted in Pefki, Greece"

Emily clicked on the link to be greeted by the white friendly smile of the female host holding a pumpkin. Emily read further.

"Hey there!

My name is Elina and I live on a beautiful Greek island of Evia. I decided to move out from the city and create a farm. I have already acres of olive trees for oil. I have made chicken and rabbit hutches, planted fig trees, grapes, blackberries, raspberries and many more. I have also built beehives to make honey.

My vision is to be as much self-sustainable as possible, so any person with that kind of vision is more than welcome. I have some projects to be done with cement like a pizza oven, an outdoor fireplace and paint the outside surface of the house.

We will plant seeds and trees all year long. We will also look for organic matter in the forest or gather mushrooms, wild fruit or herbs. We will harvest fruit for winter, olives for oil in November, grapes for wine in September, figs in August.

We will gather and chop wood for the stove through winter, create raised beds for planting organic seeds and make compost!

My interests except from these are cycling, yoga, rock climbing, the sea and cooking.

Work here, may be hard, but will be fun, educational and rewarding as well as being surrounded by strong minded women in a safe sanctuary for us to talk over our past.

If you fancy a change and feel this is for you please contact me. We are taking on new residents throughout winter."

The thought of being there at that moment sounded blissful. To be back under the Greek sunshine and surrounded by just women made it even more appealing. Emily felt a desire to be there so strong that she could not stop herself from reacting. She pressed on the contact button and sent her interest and reasons via email without a second thought.

It took just two days for her to receive a response from the host, Elina. Opening up the email, Emily's heart raced with excitement as she saw the acceptance of her offer to volunteer. The host had offered her a minimum stay of just a week to see if it was something that she would enjoy. The stay was due to commence in just two weeks time, just in time for the olive harvest.

Emily beamed as she rushed downstairs to tell her parents her news.

"Are you sure you are up to this after everything that has happened. Your ribs have still not recovered and the doctor said that it would be stupid to do anything too physical?" her mother protested.

"It is exactly what I need. This is a chance to get away for just a while. Being here just allows me to go over and over everything that has happened and it is not allowing me to move on," Emily challenged. "I am stuck in day after day with nothing to occupy my mind. No job, no income, nothing but the same cycle everyday. At least here I would be able to focus on the work, learn new skills and meet new people. You know how much I loved living in Greece. I sometimes wish that I had never returned home. It would be like returning to my childhood dream," she announced.

Emily's Mum stayed silent for a few moments as she considered her daughters words.

"And when did she say you could stay?" her mother said feeling a little apprehensive and protective at the idea of letting her daughter go.

"In just two weeks time. I really need this Mum. I can always come back after the first week if I don't like it!" she reminded her.

"Okay. Fine. Book your flight and make sure you take out some insurance. If you think this will help then I am happy to cover the costs," she reluctantly agreed.

"Something tells me it is going to be the best decision I ever made!" and with that Emily headed upstairs to confirm her arrival and book a one way ticket. Emily just knew that she wouldn't be coming back.

Two weeks seemed to take forever. Emily had packed and unpacked her suitcase several times before finally deciding on the right clothes to take. Winter in Greece brought changeable weather and it wasn't always the sunshine that most people saw in the glossy travel magazines. The last winter she had spent with Tom had been very stormy, wet and even brought some snow to the caps of the mountains surrounding their village.

Making sure that she packed some extra thermals, her mittens and a woolly hat, Emily sat firmly on her suitcase, stuffed in the bit of material that spilled out and zipped up its bulging contents. Dragging the dead weight down the stairs, she had hugged her mother goodbye after she had pushed an envelope of cash into her hand for "emergencies". Emily then jumped into the passenger seat next to her father and watched as her mother became smaller and smaller as they made their way towards the airport.

They drove through the centre of town, passing by her old flat where she saw Tammy's car parked outside. She and Colin must have hooked up after their brief meeting, Emily considered with a smile and shook her head at the brashness of her dear friend. Then she saw the alleyway where Jake had attacked her. This sent a shiver of fear through her body as she remembered his hot breathe against her face. Feeling her heart rate increase and beads of sweat form on her forehead, Emily had felt the memory of the attack consume her thoughts like a thick mist. Closing her eyes, she breathed in deeply as she slowly counted to five before exhaling the memory to the count of eight as she had seen on one of the many online support videos for assault victims. To her surprise, it had actually worked. She had completely forgotten about her momentary relapse and had successfully evaded a mild panic attack.

The journey had taken a little under an hour. Emily thanked and kissed her father goodbye, grabbed the handle of her suitcase and, with it dragging at her heels, she made her way inside the terminal building. The airport was a hive of activity with people rushing here and there. She navigated around the crowds of travellers and their suitcase filled trollies that often replicated a giant game of jenga, as they balanced precariously on top of each other. They were often topped with a small child crowning the pile as an anchor pinning them all together and stopping the cases from toppling onto the floor. Scanning the digital information board, Emily located her flight to Athens and made her way towards the allocated check in desk.

After waiting in a queue for a short while, she had grabbed her suitcase with both hands, made a hopeful swing with all her strength wishing the case to land successfully on the weighing belt. Offering her passport and ticket confirmation to the smiling check in attendant, Emily had watched in hope as the scales flickered on the screen and settled just a gram below the allowance imit. The attendant printed the label, stuck it around the handle and wished Emily a good journey.

Emily headed towards the security gates. Scanning her boarding card, she followed the line of fellow travellers along the winding retractable belt-lined path and waited her turn to filled the grey tray with all her belongings. Taking off all her jewellery, adding her boots, belt and mobile to the tray, Emily walked through the body scanner and, without a single beep, she had made it through feeling accomplished.

Redressing herself and collecting her belongings, she wandered through duty free and spent a little while testing the perfumes, noting a few favourites to add to her Christmas list for her parents to buy her as a gift. Emily became tired of the duty free and her lack of available funds to buy anything regardless. She was pretty sure that her mother would not agree that Dior sunglasses were a necessary emergency purchase.

Settling for just a hot chocolate with whipped cream and marshmallows from the airport cafe, she took out the snack box that her mother had lovingly prepared for her journey. Pulling out a chocolate Wagon Wheel, Emily took a seat, took out her book and waited for her flight gate number to be called. She lost herself in the pages of the romantic fiction almost immediately, almost wishing that she could find her own dreamy Greek fisherman named Nikolas.

After a while of being lost in a world of romance, the Athens flight was called and Emily made her way to the gate along with the wave of other travellers that appeared to rush ahead hoping to be the first in the embarkation queue. Emily's stomach suddenly tightened as she felt her confidence suddenly diminish. Was she doing the right thing by running away? What if she didn't get along with the host? What if she was attacked in a different country? What if this was all fake and another one of Jakes ploys? So many questions filtered through her mind. She didn't have to get on the plane. She could still turn around at that point and head home. Then, as if her friend had almost known that she was having doubts, a message from Tammy beeped through her device.

"You got this girl! Have the best time and just try to relax. Who knows, I could come meet you after the exams! Love you and I'm gonna miss your face! T XX"

Emily smiled and felt her body relax. She did have this. She could do anything she wanted and she would not let Jake ruin the rest of her life! Emily handed her boarding pass and passport to the smiling stewardess, settled in the waiting area ready to board the aircraft.

Chapter 14

Spiritual Home

Emily was woken by the sunrise that was just starting to penetrate through the teal blue wooden shutters that covered both bedroom windows. She lay in bed for a little while and allowed herself a moment to come around. The bed was so comfortable and she had slept so well after the long taxi journey from the airport. Checking her watch, she noted that it was just after 7am. She was due downstairs to meet with the host and other residents within the hour.

Emily took in her new surroundings. The only sounds she could hear were the birds happily singing their morning song from outside. Inside was just as calm. The walls were painted a peaceful dove grey to compliment the external ambience. Soft white voiles hung from wooden curtain rail's that delicately framed the two windows. A small dressing table sat against the wall to her left with a pretty hand drawn art mural of an olive branch surrounded by dragonflies and birds graced the wall behind the mirror. A comfortable armchair, with a single cheerful stripy cushion, welcomingly sat in the corner, next to dressing table, and looked out through the largest of the two windows.

An ample built in wardrobe filled the wall at the base of the bed and another smaller window looked out to the side of the property on her right. A white textured cloth, draped from a hoop above her and was tied up with an elegant golden sash secured against the wall behind the bed. Two bedside tables stood either side of her with dainty lamps topped with white wicker shades to match the central light that hung above. A vase of autumnal coloured dried flowers gave a burst of artificial warmth to the room.

The room was very modern in style, clean, fresh and very welcoming. It was nothing that she had expected from her previous stay in Greece. Emily threw back the crisp sheets and placed her feet onto the warm beige ceramic tiles. Even the floor gave comfort and a warming calmness to finish off the room. It was just perfect. Emily pushed herself up and wandered to the window next to the armchair. Throwing open the shutters, she was gifted by the magical elevated views of the deep blue crystal clear waters of the Aegean Sea. She took a deep breath and inhaled the citrus scent of the pine trees that floated in with the mountain breeze, intoxicating the room even more.

Emily walked towards her suitcase that she had abandoned on the bedroom floor on her late arrival before flopping into bed, exhausted by her trip. Dragging it across the warm tiles, she struggled with its weight as she lifted it onto the mattress. Unzipping the compact contents, she rummaged through her belongings to find a towel and her wash bag. Then, stepping out of her room, she wandered the brightly lit hallway in search of the toilet.

Locating the bathroom, Emily knocked gently before pushing the door open and locking it behind her. Even the bathroom was decorated in a contemporary way with its modern sink unit and retro style wall tiles. Hidden behind a glass block wall she found the shower that looked as if a whole ruby team could have joined her. Dropping her robe, she turned on the overhead power shower. The warm jet spray teased her skin with its welcoming shoulder massage as she lathered up the soap and cleansed her body. Having spent a few delicious moments under the warm water, Emily stepped out and headed back to her room to get dressed and ready for her morning.

Making her way down the wooden staircase, she followed the sound of chattering that was coming from the rear of the building. Emily found a group of women with a variety of accents, all helping out in the kitchen to create a communal breakfast. The smell of freshly baked bread filled the air as an older lady holding a basket approached her and introduced herself.

"Kalimera! I hope you slept well? My name is Elina and I wish to welcome you to my home. Everybody, this is Emily. She will be staying with us for a while," she said, introducing her to the group of ladies that had all stopped what they were doing, and stood smiling at their new colleague. "Please make yourself at home and I am sure everyone will introduce themselves over breakfast. Just jump in and help where you can!" Elina smiled, and headed to the table with the basket of warm fresh bread that she had held in her hand.

Emily wandered over to the counter where a small lady with plaited almost white blonde hair, was cutting up a large watermelon.

"Can I help you with anything?" she enquired.

"Hi Emily! My name is Aoife. It is good to meet with you! I am here from Sweden and I stay for a few more weeks yet. If you could cut up some of the oranges into slices this will be good!" she smiled as she continued to slice the watermelon on the grey granite worktops that sat on top of the bespoke wooden units.

Emily looked around the kitchen area. It was fully equipped with all the mod cons needed to cook up a meal for a large group of people yet in a very minimal contemporary design.

"Its good to meet you too Aoife! I am hoping to be a here for most of winter and maybe into next season if things work out well," Emily as she took a few of the oranges from the fruit bowl. "How many should I cut up? How many are we expecting for breakfast?" she enquired.

"There are now ten of us for breakfast including yourself. This will make the harvest much quicker when we get into the fields!" Aoife nodded. "It is so good to have fresh energy as it gets very tiring with the long days. We have to get the olives ready for the oil press before the end of November and with over 1000 trees to harvest this is not an easy task with just a few hands." She continued.

Emily knew exactly what she meant. She had spent a whole month picking olives with Tom on the mainland and after a few days her palms had been sore with blisters. She filled up a glass bowl with the oranges and followed Aoife to the table.

Taking a seat at the larger than normal farmhouse table, Emily took in the room around her. It was painted in an deep ochre yellow that reached up to the exposed wooden beams above making it feel spacious. There was a set of glazed wooden French doors that led out onto a veranda that gave a breath taking views across the calm sea.

The rest of the ladies had taken a seat at the table and, before they started their meal, Elina held out both her hands and took her neighbours hands, which created a chain reaction amongst the group. Emily mimicked everyone and reluctantly took the hand of the strangers sat either side of her until they had created a complete interlinked circle. Emily watched as everyone closed their eyes and sat in silence for a few moments before breaking apart and bursting into chatter again.

Breakfast smelt divine and was so delicious. The table had burst with colour from the selection of delicious fruits that were sliced, diced or piled up in the centre. Along with the yeasty smell of the warm crusty bread, was a selection of pungent cheeses, cold cuts of meat, olives, marmalades, eggs and sweet Greek pastries. There were a variety of herbal drinks plus plenty of strong punchy Greek coffee to thrust the tiredest of minds into a frenzy of energy.

Taking her third coffee of the morning, Emily followed Elina onto the veranda and felt her first rays of the autumn Greek sunshine warm her cheeks with its welcoming touch. The sea vista from the veranda was spectacular. It looked out towards the mainland to one side and the island of Skiathos in the distance. Emily could see a small village further down the hill nestled in amongst the verdant green pine trees that filled the landscape before her and almost fell into the crystal clear sea. A small fishing harbour lay close to a long narrow beach. It seemed well organised with lines of sunbeds and umbrella's ready for any last minute sun seekers reluctant to give in on the changing seasons.

"Welcome to Pefki, home of all the pine trees on Evia!" Elina said as she linked her arm through a mesmerised Emily's and pulled her close. "It is pretty, no? Please, come and I shall walk you through our gardens."

Elina led Emily down some steps that led into the established gardens that surrounded the villa.

"Your home is just beautiful Elina!" Emily exclaimed. "I thought that I would be coming to a traditional Greek home with run down buildings and shack accommodation for me to sleep in and not the luxury that I have seen so far," she announced.

"Thank you. The villa is a very modern bioclimatic design, meaning it is built with its environment in mind. It was built to utilize the solar energy to heat the inside effectively by trapping the heat inside. It is protected by these large orange and lemon trees through summer," she paused pointing at four large fruit trees that loomed above them.

"These shade the villa from the heat of the strong Greek summer sun, and along with the smaller windows on this side of the property they keep it cool, creating a healthy and inviting living space. They also provide us with delicious food that we can pick and enjoy through summer!" she smiled. "This is my aim, to live in harmony with the natural surroundings and to educate people who stay to make use of what we have instead of installing wasteful air conditioning units that use harmful fossil fuels, which is not really needed," Elina continued. "We heat the home with additional solar panels found on the roof and use any fallen trees from our gardens in our open fire for extra heat during the coldest months, but this is not always necessary."

They wandered through a few olive trees that lined a dust path towards a glimmering kidney shaped swimming pool that seemed to touch the sea and skyline. The shrubs and trees enclosed the sun patio from view, giving the pool area complete privacy from the house. A small barbeque area sat in the far corner and a few sun loungers dotted the perimeter of the pool.

"The pool is not heated and just relies of the sun to warm it through the summer months. We are now starting to lose the heat of the sun as autumn is in full swing so only the brave dare to take a dip!" Elina smiled.

Emily could smell the intensity of the resin of the pine trees that filled the air with its sweet citrus aroma, the further they walked into the gardens. Teasing glimmers of the deep blue Aegean sea burst through the olive trees that filled the remainder of the gardens. The pungent warming medicinal scent of thyme crunched under her feet spewing out wafts of the essence of Greece that she knew and loved.

"We have over four acres of Olive groves here which are now ready for early harvest to create the olive oil at the local frantoio to be processed. This will be the hard work we have for the next few weeks as we have found that picking them traditionally by hand is the best way. If you survive the first week and wish to stay, then there is work to build a pizza oven and repaint the exterior of the house before the rains come. This area isn't green for no reason!" Elina advised. "Today I will put you with Aoife who is a long term resident here and is good to learn from. She will help you to get to know the ropes, as you say!"

"I am in awe of your home Elina. It has been a long time since I was in Greece. I am sure I will love it here! How many will work in the fields for the harvest this season?" Emily enquired.

"We have the ladies who all live at the villa, which is now ten plus we have a few locals that will come to help. But it is not all work here. We do have some time to enjoy the island. You will be able to use the car on the weekends to drive along the coast to the thermal spa's and waterfalls that North Evia is famous for, plus, of course, just a few meters below and a pretty walk through the pine trees is our private beach. Artemision and port of Pefki are a short stroll away. Here you can take a swim or enjoy the taverna's. I take a yoga class on the veranda every morning at sunrise and before breakfast. If you wish to join us then please be ready by 6am," Elina smiled. "Now lets head back to the others and we shall get ready for the harvest!"

Chapter 15

Healing Waters

Emily's neck and arms ached. Taking her rake above her, she fought through the pain of her ribs and hit at the overhead branches for the hundredth time that day. A shower of green and black olives dropped to the floor onto the netting purposely placed beneath her feet to catch the precious harvest. With her housemates all circled around the ancient tree, they attacked it gently from all sides relieving it of its annual bounty.

One of the young local boys, Panos, had scaled it's twisted trunk and pruned the higher branches, sending them crashing to the floor to be stripped of their fruits. Having completely removed all the olives from her section of the tree, Emily picked up one of the pruned branches that was laden and heavy with fruit. Using the handle of her rake, she beat at the branch, until all the olives had fallen to her feet. The work was physically tiring yet it had an element of satisfaction watching the hard work of the team result in a successful harvest. This was only the ninth tree that had assaulted that day and it was already after midday.

Elina had arrived with the welcoming sight of lunch just as they were bagging up the last of that mornings harvest into the large hessian sacks and stacking then onto the back of the trailer. Throwing her rack to the floor, Emily sank, like a heavy weight, to the floor alongside an exhausted Danish lady named Imogen, who was on a gap year from her studies. Emily had now been in Pefki for a week and, even though she was still the new girl, had managed to forge a friendship with almost all her housemates.

Reaching forward to take a slice of bread and very welcoming herbal tea, Emily took a mouthful of the warming liquid. The burst of peppermint refreshed her palate and warmed her hands against the mug. The air was starting to become colder as November had arrived. The heat from the sunshine was not as harsh but it still filled the sky endlessly from dusk until dawn. Emily had not yet witnessed a dark cloudy day or the torrential rains that she had been warned to expect. Leaning against the trunk of the olive tree behind her, she looked up through the canopy at the deep blue cloudless sky and was grateful for a moments shade. Emily considered what the weather would have been back at home at that very moment. The thought of the damp grey British weather made her shudder.

Just another few more olive trees to go until the weekend would begin. She had made plans with Aoife to travel to the thermal spa's of Edipsos the following day, of which she had been assured would soothe her aching muscles and joints. The thought of any respite from the long days working relentlessly in the olive fields seemed like bliss. Emily had not done physical work in so long, that she had ached in places that she didn't even know had existed. This was a far cry from her vocal career although the days in the gardens did bring sporadic moments of group singing to lighten the workload.

However, the hard physical work had also not allowed her a moment to think about her ordeal with Jake. It had absorbed every ounce of concentration. This had seemed to be the best remedy for her state of mind. She had a daily purpose and reason to get up and face her challenges here in Greece. Back in the UK she had no purpose or reason for anything. Too much time to think and dwell on her past had not been a healthy decision.

Having filled her stomach with a delicious plate of feta, olives and salad, along with eggs and grilled sardines, Emily felt nourished and ready for the afternoon shift. Taking her rake, she pushed herself from the ground and followed the others to the next tree.

The following morning, Emily was up before sunrise. She had taken a shower and was already sat on a yoga mat embracing the first of the suns rays as it rose over the watery horizon. A couple of the other ladies had also arrived and taken a seated position on the floor ahead of the regular morning session.

Elina arrived and took her usual crossed legged position facing the sunrise at the front of the group.

"Ladies, whilst we wait for the others to arrive, lets start by taking in some of the morning air, deep into our lungs. Let the new day fill you with its hope and wonder," she said as she placed her arms loosely on her knees, straightened her back and closed her eyes. Emily followed suit and shut her eyes. She breathed in the invigorating scent of the surrounding pine. The morning air was so refreshing that it bit cold at her nose as she sat in the stillness. The waves breaking on the shale below, seemed to create a lulling beat for her to follow with her breathing. A few birds had begun to sing their dawn chorus from their surrounding treetop roosts. The moment was so hypnotic that she felt herself fall deep into the meditation of the moment.

Her body became relaxed and her mind heard nothing but the serenity of nature around her. The sun had started to warm the morning air and bathed them all in its golden glow as it rose above the sea before them. Following Elina's lead after a few minutes of self indulgence, Emily stood, taking care to rise from her pose gently so not to loose balance. Standing tall for a few moments she started the sun salutation routine, alongside the rest of the group. She had begun to enjoy this gentle start to the day, as it seemed to relax her thoughts and ease any anxieties that may have shrouded her from another restless night.

Even though she was safely away from the reminders of her ordeal, Emily was still woken by terrifying night terrors that always took her back to that moment in the darkness of the alleyway. If she allowed herself, she could still feel the roughness of Jakes unshaven face and his hot breathe across her cheeks. She would often be woken by an animated fight with an invisible attacker, covered in beads of sweat and frozen stiff with fear. Then, unable to return to sleep, memories of the attack and her relationship with Jake had filled every corner of her mind. It was almost as if she was trying to get closure on her ordeal yet had no answers to his reason for wanting to destroy her sanity and desire to kill her.

After the hour long Yoga session, Emily felt her stomach rumble in hunger. She had lost quite a bit of weight since arriving and not having the ability to snack through boredom. Here, there was never a moment spare as chores and work had to be done in order for the day to run smoothly. Chickens needed cleaning, goats needed milking and crops needed harvesting so that they ate that evening. She was active for most of the day and only rested when they ate or slept.

But today, being Saturday, was her rest day. This was her first day of doing nothing since arriving on Evia and she had plans to be a tourist that day. After eating a filling breakfast, Emily headed to her room, packed a rucksack with her towel and bathers and met with a grinning Aoife in the kitchen.

"So are we set to go, yes?" Aoife enquired.

"All set! I really looking forward to this!" Emily replied, realising that this would actually be the first time she had away from the villa since arriving.

"Lets get going then! It doesn't take too long before we arrive!" Aoife said, taking Emily's arm.

Emily followed Aoife through the door and to the small communal car that was parked under the shade of an orange tree.

She opened the car door and threw her bag onto the rear seat before settling into the passenger seat and securing her seatbelt.

Aoife had made herself comfortable in the driver seat and turned the ignition making the dusty car burst to life. With in seconds, they were following the coastal road towards the north west of the island. The views over the Aegean sea were mesmerising. The different hues of the water ranged from a vibrant turquoise-green in the shallows to a deeper blue. The sea palate complimented the clear skies above perfectly. The sun was already warm on her arm as she rested it on the open window of the car.

Emily pushed her sunglasses off the top of her head and secured them over the bridge of her nose and lent her head against the car door. She breathed in the pleasant morning air as Aoife turned on the radio that blasted out an uplifting traditional Greek tune. This was how she had remembered her previous time in Greece. The music sent a shiver of goosebumps down her arm, as those distant memories flooded back bringing a wide smile across her face.

Forgotten nights in mountain village taverns, serenaded by the chirps of cicadas hidden in the wild sage and thyme that intoxicated the night with their heady aroma. Drinking copious amounts of the potent pine infused retsina whilst sat under a swagger of festoon lights, strung loosely from one fig tree to another as an elderly Greek man had played his violin as nimble as any youngster and another plucked swiftly at his bouzouki, as if he had been born with it attached to his fingers. Hypnotised by their timeless melody, Emily would watch as the villagers gathered in an entwined circle and performed their traditional regional dances in perfection.

Those were times when she had felt most alive and connected to everything around her. Everything was so simple yet she had burst with so much gratitude and happiness. There had been no internet to distract her from reality. It was a time when she had to learn to socialise and communicate using her own instincts to get by. Now it seemed life had become disengaged. All she needed to do was type in her needs to Google and everything was done for her. There was little need to learn any language or want to socialise with the locals now. Everything she needed to learn about Greece and its traditions was right in her pocket and at the touch of her finger. If she had wanted bouzouki, she just searched it on Youtube. But Emily had soaked up every bit of the culture that she could during her previous stay and had left missing the Greek way of life.

The road had taken them away from the coast and through miles of farmed pastures before reaching the built up town of Istiaia. As they drove through the town, Emily noted its modern look. Cafes and shops lined the streets filled with busy shoppers going about their day. They reached the edge of the town and passed by the hospital before heading back out in the Greek countryside. The road started to climb upwards into a small range of mountain filled with pine trees that briefly skirted the coast before again heading inland and descending through a cluster of small mountain hamlets towards the distant glimmers of the Aegean.

As the sea gradually became closer and they started the drive down through the pine and eucalyptus trees that filled the air with their medicinal aroma and towards Edipsos. Emily noted a typical traditional Greek coastal village that skirted the clear blue waters. Some of the buildings looked as if they were from the previous century but a few modern looking hotels sat prominently close to the seemingly steaming sea water.

Parking the car, Emily stepped out and immediately noted the distinct eggy smell of sulphur in the air. Reaching into retrieve her bag, she followed an eager Aoife as she navigated her way silently through the town centre. The street was lined with tavernas and cafes that followed along the shore. Groups of older people sat and watched the boats going back and forth to the mainland that could be seen in the distance.

The welcoming smell of deep fried loukomades wafted through the air as they passed a young child with the biggest grin as his mother drizzled honey over the sweet treat. It smelt reminiscent of the donut stall at the fairgrounds she had visited as a child with her grandparents and left her yearning for a plate topped with thick creamy Greek yoghurt. They passed by a small stream that sent wafts of steam up into the air as it flowed past. Emily must have been pulling a confused expression on her face as Aoife suddenly broke the silence.

"There are so many hot springs around Edipsos that feed into the swimming pools and hot tubs of the hotels that we are passing. This is the most amazing resort in Greece with around eighty different springs with water ranging in temperature from warm to very hot. People come from all around the world to bath in these waters as they belief they cure almost every ailment including sexual problems for men and ladies. Even the sea is hotter here as warm water gushes from geezers deep beneath the seabed making it an all year round spa resort. And the best thing is they are completely free!" Aoife smiled.

As they made their way closer to the beach, Emily could see people bathing in the steaming hot water which poured through various crevices or cascaded down from the rocks above and showering the visitors with its steamy hot waters, leaving multi-colour streaked sediment in strange formations on the landscape above.

Placing her bag on the golden shale and sand floor, Emily pulled out her towel and slipped it around her waist. Clutching at it precariously, she slipped off her jeans and knickers with her free hand, then, discarded them to the side as she balanced on one leg to step into her swimsuit. The yoga lessons had seemingly paid off, as the process was not as painful as she had remembered from her past. Dropping the towel to the floor, she gathered her clothes and placed them into her rucksack. Aoife had already made her way into the almost empty sea and was floating on her back.

Emily carefully navigated her way to the waters edge through the sea-smoothed pebbles that lay scattered on the sand, until she reached the tepid Aegean waters. This would be her first swim in the salty teal green waters. Making her way into the shallows, the water was almost unbearably cold until she felt a warm current coming from the bed beneath her. She sank herself into the warming flow and enjoyed its relief momentarily before she felt it disburse into the colder seawater. Emily continued to swim until she felt another burst of warm water from below her almost as if someone had turned on the hot tap in her bath.

"It's quite crazy here!" Emily shouted to Aoife who had made her way towards a plateau of rocks that were scattered with a few other bathers who were enjoying the hot springs.

"Come, there are a few empty pools here for us to enjoy!" Aoife suggested, as Emily swam to join her.

The rocks here looked uninviting and as if they had mouldy cheese melted over the top. Pulling herself up onto the plateau, she wandered towards one of the manmade pool that was being constantly filled with a steaming spring that was gushing through the surrounding sea wall, almost like a jacuzzi. Stepping into the rock pool, Emily lowered herself into its welcoming hot waters and rested her head against the strange rock formations behind her. She closed her eyes as she felt the gushing warm waters instantly soothe her aching back and shoulders. Emily felt as if she had been thrust back in time to ancient Greece.

After a while of delicious self indulgence, Emily opened her eyes, pushed herself into a sitting position and scanned the horizon. The skyline was endless and the calmness of her surroundings was just what she had needed at that moment. She noted the majestic pine clad hills that skirted the village and rolled gently to the shore, with a few terracotta topped luxury hotels cut into the hillside, fighting for the best vistas over the small bay.

Emily looked towards the cascade of water that was falling over the rocks and into the sea just a little further around the bay. The spring water seemed to be providing a hot shower over a young man who was stood alone and enjoying the surreal moment beneath its hot spray. She watched as he raised his arms and brushed his jet-black hair back from his face, exposing a perfectly tanned and toned physique. His physique looked familiar and had reminded her of someone she had once known. Shaking the thought from her mind, Emily continued to watch him bathe. The moment was quite reminiscent of a TV advert that she had voiced over for a tropical brand of shampoo. She smiled as she continued to watch the man enjoying the moment. He must have noticed her watching as he threw her a wide smile and dived beneath the seawater, emerging a few meters from the shore.

She watched as he swam for a while, throwing her a few white smiles and cheeky glances before emerging from the water at waist height and seemed to swagger through the water towards her. Emily looked around to see if he was walking towards someone else, but apart from Aoife, they were alone.

"Do you know him?" Emily questioned towards Aoife.

Shaking her head and shrugging her shoulders, Emily continued to observe him as he approached. The closer he came, the more familiar he looked. Emily was confused. How could this possibly be? Emily's heart felt a sudden sharp pang. She immediately knew that she had meant to go through everything she had to be were she was right that second. She knew in that instant that this was her destiny and she was never going back to the UK. As stood just a few feet from her, smiling like a Cheshire cat and looking even better than she had remembered was her biggest regret and the love of her life, Tom.